The Legacy of Merton Manor

The Legacy of
Merton Manor

Dorothy Brenner Francis

Thorndike Press • Chivers Press
Waterville, Maine USA   Bath, England

This Large Print edition is published by Thorndike Press, USA and by Chivers Press, England.

Published in 2003 in the U.S. by arrangement with Maureen Moran Agency.

Published in 2003 in the U.K. by arrangement with the author.

U.S. Hardcover 0-7862-5071-2 (Candlelight Series)
U.K. Hardcover 0-7540-8920-7 (Chivers Large Print)
U.K. Softcover 0-7540-8921-5 (Camden Large Print)

The text of this Large Print edition is unabridged.
Other aspects of the book may vary from the original edition.

Set in 16 pt. Plantin by Al Chase.

Printed in the United States on permanent paper.

British Library Cataloguing-in-Publication Data available

Library of Congress Cataloging-in-Publication Data

Francis, Dorothy Brenner.
    The legacy of Merton Manor / Dorothy Brenner Francis.
      p. cm.
    ISBN 0-7862-5071-2 (lg. print : hc : alk. paper)
    1. Cornwall (England : County) — Fiction.
  2. Housekeepers — Fiction. 3. Manors — Fiction.
  4. Large type books. I. Title.
  PS3556.R327 L44 2003
   813′.54—dc21   2002038433

The Legacy of
Merton Manor

CHAPTER ONE

I awakened to the horror of my own screaming. My fingers groped for the locket. It was there. He hadn't taken it. But how silly! He was only part of my terrible nightmares.

"Margo! Are you all right?"

Julia rushed into my room.

"Y-yes. I'm all right." I sat up. "I'm sorry to have awakened you — again."

"This can't go on, Margo. You'll have a breakdown. Was it the same nightmare?"

"Yes. The tall silver-haired man with the black eyebrows stood at my bedside." I shuddered. "His eyes stare into mine until I feel hypnotized. Then he says, 'Drop it in my hand,' and when I reach for the locket, I wake up screaming."

"I'll make tea," Julia said. "That'll settle your nerves."

I watched Julia go. I liked this distant cousin of my father's. She was like an old-fashioned underwear button: direct, sturdy, and useful. I always knew where I stood with Julia.

Slipping into a robe, I paced about my

small basement apartment. So much had happened that I couldn't control that I had almost given up fighting. But now, in the aftermath of a nightmare, a theme from one of my college term papers droned through my mind: We are constantly called upon to create our own futures. I wished the words would stop haunting me. Now, alone and shaken, my goal of becoming a writer seemed impossible to attain. I could only drift with currents that were sweeping me into the unknown.

"Here. Drink this." Julia returned and set a cup of tea on my desk and motioned me into a chair. "It will calm you."

I sat and sipped the tea, but tears sprang to my eyes.

"Don't cry, Margo. The nightmare's over. Forget it."

"I wasn't crying over the nightmare. It's this house. How my parents dreamed and planned for it! And how short a time they had to enjoy it! It's unfair!"

"Life seldom is fair," Julia said. "You have to adjust."

I stood to give authority to my words. "You're right. And I'll start my adjusting with a trip to Merton Manor."

Julia sighed. "Margo! How do you hope to help yourself by going where you know you're unwelcome?"

"I must go. I promised Mother. My procrastination is causing these nightmares. When I keep my promise, they'll go away. Look! I've already bought a travel suit."

Julia's eyes danced at the prospect of viewing new clothes as I opened the box from Bonwit's. She held up the suit.

"It's you, Margo. The color will turn your eyes into blue sapphires, and you're tall and slim enough to carry the bulk of the fabric without looking thick through the middle."

Good old Julia! My mirror told me how plain I was, yet Julia had never mentioned my eagle's beak of a nose or my arrow-pointed chin. Somehow she managed to make me see only my good points. But the new clothes distracted Julia only momentarily.

"No one should be held to a deathbed promise, Margo. It's unfair. You survived the car crash, your parents' deaths. Don't punish yourself further by trying to keep an impossible promise."

"I can't keep on driving myself crazy. I didn't resign from my job at the publishing house, Julia. Mr. Reist fired me. But he said he'd rehire me when my health improved."

"Then see a doctor," Julia said. "Don't go to Cornwall."

Julia snapped off the light as she left my

9

room, but I lay wide awake. I had to go to Cornwall. And who besides Julia would care? Certainly not Ralph. Ralph Dawson had neither called nor written to me for weeks. A young executive needs a wife who can enhance his social position. Ralph didn't need me.

"Cornwall." I whispered the exotic word. I often had wondered what my mother's childhood home was like. Slipping from bed, I went to my desk and snatched my Aunt Katherine's well-worn letter from my stationery kit.

Merton Manor
Bodrevy Village
Cornwall, England
March 1

Miss Margo Landon
126 Brighton Road
Plainview, New York

Dear Miss Landon:

Your letter has been received at Merton Manor. I regret to inform you that Sir Henry Merton is a sick man. Please remember that. When Wanda, your mother, deserted him years ago, she was disinherited. A visit from you at this time would only worsen my father's condition.

Please do not endanger yourself by coming here, and please refrain from further correspondence.

Katherine Merton Noel

"Margo!"

Julia's voice startled me; I dropped the letter.

"I knew you were still up mooning over that letter."

"Julia, what kind of people were the Mertons?"

"I know little about them." Julia shrugged. "Sir Henry is a historian, I believe. The family was extremely wealthy."

"Did Mother ever speak to you of her sister?" I asked. "Not Katherine, but a younger sister?"

Julia paused, deep in thought. "Yes, but I can't remember her name. And I believe there was a foster brother."

I pulled the sheet up to my chin, and once more Julia left me alone. Who was Katherine to tell me what to do? My mother's wishes should certainly come first. By going to England I might be creating my own future. What did I have to lose?

In fact I had much to gain. Katherine Merton was a famous novelist noted for never having granted a personal interview to anyone. My former boss would be most impressed if I could come up with such an interview. Perhaps Katherine would relent.

I touched the locket around my neck, and my mother's last words came back to me as clearly as if she were in the room.

"Margo, take this locket to my father at Merton Manor. Don't open it. Give it to no one else. Drop it into his own hand."

"I will, Mother." I said the words aloud as I had said them that day in the hospital. "I will, Mother."

And I knew then that I would keep my promise. I was finished drifting. I would create my own future, and if danger lay ahead as Aunt Katherine had warned, then I would face it.

CHAPTER TWO

The next weeks would have been unbearable without Julia's encouragement.

"If you're determined to go to Cornwall, then the least I can do is to help you get ready." Julia began making a list.

"There's so much to be done. How can I thank you, Julia?"

"Passport. Reservations. Luggage." Julia read her list.

Shopping. Planning. Packing. I was too busy to consider the consequences of my trip to Cornwall until Julia drove me to the airport on the first of April.

"Am I an April fool?" I asked as I eyed the waiting jet.

"It's too late now for soul-searching," Julia replied. "You write to me the minute you arrive at Merton Manor."

"Of course I will," I said. "Thank you for all you've done." There was no more time for talking, as we had arrived at my flight gate. I gave Julia a hug, and then I ran for the ramp. Minutes after I found my seat, engines roared, the huge jet vibrated powerfully, and the force of the plane's takeoff pinned me against the seat.

After the stewardess completed her welcome and her instructions, the exhaustion of the past few days overtook me. I dozed or slept during most of the long flight.

The jet touched down on schedule, and as soon as I had deplaned and claimed my luggage, an airport attendant hailed a taxi for me and directed the driver to the motorcoach terminal.

The cabby sat behind the wheel of his car with the air of a squire escorting a princess to the ball. "Relax, mum. You'll soon be getting used to the traffic."

"I knew the English drove on the left side of the street," I said, "but merely knowing didn't prepare me for the actuality of it. Sir, I want to catch a bus to Bodrevy Village."

For a moment my driver didn't answer; Big Ben was chiming the hour. I listened in awe.

"You'll be finding that no buses run that far, miss," the driver said when the clock was quiet.

My heart sank. "But I must get to Bodrevy Village."

"Motor coach. You must be taking a motor coach, miss. Buses are only for local transportation."

I relaxed. Motor coach? Bus? Who cared

14

what it was called so long as it was going to Bodrevy Village! My driver was most gracious. Due to his helpfulness I had no problems in locating the green double-deck coach bound for Cornwall.

"Thank you, sir." I smiled as he pocketed my tip, but he scowled and nodded toward the coach.

"Tis a lady driver you'll be having now. Women's lib, you know." The cabby shrugged, helped me onto the coach, and left.

I studied the face of the lady coach conductor. Small boned and petite, she seemed fragile as a china figurine. Could she drive this monster across the Queen's land?

I needn't have worried. She maneuvered the coach as easily as if it were a tiny sports car. Once we were out of London, we bumped from hamlet to hamlet. Housewives got off and on. Artisans boarded the bus carrying the tools of their trade. And children with school kits laughed and scuffled with each other.

I watched the lush countryside fly by outside my window. Green hedgerows separated even greener fields. Britain was like a map divided into emerald squares. I dozed, wakened, and dozed.

"Cornwall," the driver called at last.

15

"I could have guessed as much," I said, moving to a seat near her. "This countryside lacks the softness, the gentleness that marked the counties we passed through earlier."

She nodded. "Cornwall is a harsh land."

I was the only person who left the coach at Bodrevy Village. I had planned in advance exactly what I was going to do.

"Ma'am," I said to the coach driver, "where will I be able to find someone to deliver a message to Merton Manor?"

"I'll help you." She took the envelope I held out and approached a cluster of men loitering near the coach stop. They exchanged a few words, then one dark-haired man took the letter and walked toward me.

"The Mertons are expecting you?" he asked.

I avoided his question. "I'd like to have my message delivered to Sir Henry Merton in person, no one else. If this is impossible, please return it to me." I gave the man a pound note, and he pocketed it with a grin.

"Yes, ma'am. I'll see that the letter gets to Sir Henry himself." The man got into a battered car and drove away.

I sat down on a splintered bench near the coach stop. It was late afternoon, and fog was beginning to swirl in from the sea.

16

Many people passed by, all studying me from the corners of their eyes. Fishermen. Housewives. Children with dogs and cats. I squirmed under their curious gazes.

After a long while a handsome man driving an Austin braked his car at the coach stop and alighted. He was of medium height and dressed in somber tweeds with leather patches on the elbows. He wore heavy Wellington boots, and he approached me with a purposeful stride. His mouth was wide and sensuous, but he didn't smile. His brooding look put me on guard.

"Margo Landon?"

As he spoke my name his face grew livid, and a few scattered freckles that matched his reddish-brown hair stood out like bran flakes floating in milk.

"I'm Margo Landon." I offered my hand.

"And I'm Dan Taledon, Sir Henry's son-in-law."

Dan Taledon shook my hand with a crushing grip, then dropped it immediately as if it had burned his flesh.

"Your arrival is quite a surprise," he said.

"It shouldn't be. I wrote Sir Henry that I was coming."

Dan Taledon's eyes widened in undisguised surprise, and he changed the subject. "We'll put your cases in the car straight off, and then we'll stop at the pub for a bite to eat. It's Tillie's day off at the manor. Are you starved?"

"Hungry enough." I picked up my cosmetic case and followed him to his car. Maneuvering my suitcases into the tiny vehicle was like packing baby elephants into a sardine can.

"The sharp smell of the ocean is a welcome change from the stuffiness of the motor coach," I said, "and the pulsing of the waves is soothing after being in traffic."

"You've had a hard trip," Dan said. "But you'll find Merton Manor restful."

"What beauty!" I exclaimed as Dan guided me over the cobblestones toward the pub. "Fishermen mending nets, children playing hopscotch, housewives tending babies. It's picturesque!"

"Better memorize the scene if you like it." Dan snorted. "The evening fog's already rolling in. By the time we've eaten a bit you won't be able to see anything." Dan spoke softly, yet his voice was deep and virile.

The pub was a small wooden building that fitted like a jigsaw piece into a maze of other buildings. A sign overhead proclaimed it "The Pirate's Den," and at the entrance I hung back.

"Will I be welcome in this place? I've read . . ."

"Of course you'll be welcome." Dan opened the door. "The pub's divided into two sections. The public bar serves the working men; the saloon bar serves the quality — or those who think of themselves as such."

"Which bar are we entering?"

"Let's try for the public bar. I'm sure you're quality, but the public bar is more fascinating for the newcomer."

Inside, candles and dim electric bulbs lighted a long, narrow room. The smell of burning wax mingled with cooking odors. We sat down at a rustic table near the door, and the other patrons hushed their talk and stared.

"What's the matter?" I squirmed in my chair. "Surely we're not welcome in here. We're making everyone uneasy."

"No need to whisper." Dan spoke in a normal tone, then turned and waved to the men sitting around a fireplace at one end of the room. The wave was our ticket of admission, for the men returned it, then resumed their drinking and their conversation.

"Two teas. Two cress sandwiches," Dan said to the waitress.

As I scrutinized Dan, his handsomeness

19

made me conscious of my own plainness. The color had returned to his cheeks, and the faint smell of leather hung about him. As I watched he unwrapped a Pepto disk and chewed thoughtfully on it.

"Ulcers," he explained. "Dratted nuisance."

We visited casually for a few moments, and then after the waitress brought our snack, I said, "Tell me about Merton Manor. My mother told me little about her home. If you're Sir Henry's son-in-law, then you must be married to one of my aunts."

"Angela was my wife. She died five years ago."

"Oh! I didn't know." Bread stuck in my throat, and I washed it down with a swallow of tea.

"No, I suppose not." Dan unwrapped another Pepto. "I knew nothing of your mother until solicitors informed Sir Henry of her death."

Dan kept glancing over his shoulder. I followed his gaze each time until I realized that it was just a habit.

"I'm glad you brought me into the public bar," I said, seeking a safer topic. "It's like a three-ring circus."

"The Lanner brothers come in each evening." Dan nodded toward one end of the room where five men were enjoying a noisy game of darts. "Pete and Doc are always here playing checkers, and sometimes I stop in for a game of dominoes."

I watched the pub scene until the silence between Dan and myself grew uncomfortable.

"Tell me about Sir Henry," I said. "What's he like?"

Dan gulped some tea. "He's an unusual man. Used to be tough as a hickory root, but age is telling on him. He's tall, almost six feet. His hair's silver, but his eyebrows are coal-black. Gives him an owlish look, it does. And he's wise enough to deserve such. He's a historian and a writer. Still works every day although he's in his seventies."

I shuddered as I imagined the man in my nightmares. Did I have a sixth sense? Had I already seen my grandfather in my dreams? I pushed that thought from my mind.

"And what do you do at the manor?" I asked.

"I'm your aunt Katherine's secretary. You've surely heard of your famous aunt. I serve her, and I also try to keep the business end of the manor functioning properly."

I was nonplussed. "You don't look like a secretary."

21

"And how do secretaries look?"

I felt my face flush. I couldn't put my thoughts into speech. Dan exuded masculinity and an animal magnetism that drew me to him in spite of myself.

"You're saying to yourself, 'How could he be content to serve as someone's secretary? Has he no ambitions of his own?' "

"Your job is none of my concern. I didn't mean to pry. I would find any job in the literary world fascinating." Although I hated to admit it to myself, I found that Dan's lack of personal ambition was the very thing that attracted me. After living in the circle of Ralph's driving restlessness, Dan was a welcome change.

"Are you finished?" Dan glanced at my empty plate and cup.

I nodded. "I can hardly wait to see Merton Manor."

"Why have you come here?" Dan's eyes were the color of weak tea, and he met my gaze with the look of a cornered fox, desperate and angry.

"To see my grandfather, of course." Suddenly I felt as if the locket around my neck had turned to a branding iron searing my skin. Somehow every word I uttered had a way of disturbing Dan Taledon. I had been forcing him to talk. Almost all his words had been in answer to direct questions. We walked to the Austin. Dan held the door for me, then walked to the driver's side and slid under the wheel.

"The fog's sweeping in," Dan commented.

"The village is beautiful," I said. I admired a row of bungalows, each with its own fenced-off garden jeweled with pinks and lavender. Each house had a sign bearing its name, and I read these with amusement and interest.

" 'Journey's End.' 'At Last Ours.' 'End of the Rainbow.' This village sounds like one step from paradise."

Dan scowled and accelerated the Austin, and we drove up a steep cobblestone path that wound to the top of the cliff. The area was deserted except for some hares that frolicked on the moorland. I resolved to match Dan's silence.

The fog was like dirty cream on the clifftop, and I soon forgot my vow of silence. "How will you ever be able to see the road ahead? It's no more than a lane and . . ."

"There are landmarks." Dan nodded to our right, where a tall black column pointed skyward.

"What's that?" I blurted.

"The ruins from the old copper-mining

industry," Dan replied. "You'll see some roofless engine houses, too. Wheal Betsy has collapsed, and Wheal Charlotte is an empty shell. The word *wheal* means workplace, a place where men used to work."

Dan seemed to want to play tour guide. Perhaps he found speaking of the countryside more comfortable than speaking of the Mertons. In the distance I saw a stone house, square and rugged, but I didn't mention it. It disappeared in the fog.

"This moorland's like a cake of Swiss cheese," Dan said. "It's riddled with holes — mine shafts. The fog hides them now, and even in sunlight they are sometimes hidden behind thorn and groser." He shifted gears and continued speaking. "Of course, Cornwall has always been noted for its tin. But copper contributed far more to the wealth of Cornwall than tin. The copper mines were richer, and there were more of them."

"Did you know anyone who worked the mines?" I asked.

"No Mertons. But some of the Lanrith ancestors did. That's their house up ahead. It's hidden by fog now, but you'll see it tomorrow. The family works for Sir Henry now."

Just then the Austin gave a sickening

lurch and slid to a stop with the right rear end sagging alarmingly.

"Flat tire?" I opened my door and peered into the fog.

"Close the door and stay in the car." Dan revved the motor, and I heard the scream of spinning tires.

"We're in a bloody mire." Dan opened his door. "I must have missed the damned jog somewhere along the way."

Dan revved the motor again. We sank deeper into the mire.

"But it didn't look muddy," I said, wondering if Dan had done this deliberately to frighten me. I remembered Aunt Katherine's letter and its mention of danger. I shuddered.

"This moor is full of bogs." Dan sighed. "There's nothing to do now but walk for help."

I opened my car door again.

"Not you," Dan said. "I'll go. I'll try not to be long. But you wait. Do you understand? Don't leave the car."

"If you're sure . . ." I murmured. I didn't want to wait here in this dank grayness alone. Neither did I want to be a burden to Dan as he went for help, if that was really where he was going. But I had no choice. I had to obey Dan's order. How I wished I had listened to Julia and stayed home!

Dan carried a flashlight, but its beam soon disappeared from sight, and I sat alone peering into the swirling darkness. I was uneasy, but I wasn't really frightened until a doleful howling wavered across the moor. The hound of the Baskervilles? I tried to make jokes in my mind, but my teeth began to chatter. Had Dan gone for help? Or had he deliberately abandoned me on a desolate moor?

CHAPTER THREE

I locked the door on the Austin and hunched down in the seat. The howling continued, the fog grew thicker, and night wrapped me in a bone-gripping chill. After a long time I shivered and squinted at the luminous dial on my watch. Nine o'clock.

An hour later my nagging qualms mounted an escalator of fear. Perhaps I was being unfair to think Dan was trying to frighten me. Had something happened to him? I thought of the moorland, of the mine shafts waiting to trap their unsuspecting victims.

I waited another quarter of an hour before I left the car. Ten-fifteen! I felt sure that something had happened to Dan, and I felt duty bound to try to help. The car was headed toward the old house I had seen in the distance. I stood for a moment by the right headlight trying to get my bearings. Here the ground was firm underfoot. Surely I could reach the house safely.

"Dan!" I shouted into the fog. No answer.

The howling came from a great distance; I was in no immediate danger of being attacked by the animal involved.

"Dan! Dan!" At intervals I shouted his name. Still no answer. Walking through the fog was like easing through moist cobwebs. I kept trying to brush the eerie veil from my face. Caution slowed my progress until suddenly I felt as if hundreds of fangs were probing the flesh of my legs.

"Yeiii . . ." I stifled a scream. In a moment common sense told me I had blundered into a thorn bush.

Moments later I stepped into the mire as I tried to go around the brier patch. I had tested the ground and it had felt solid enough, then the crust crunched, crumbled, and gave away, and I sank into the ooze. I pulled my foot from the slime, losing my shoe in the process. Somehow that shoe seemed important. I groped in the cold slick muck with my hand until I felt it and pulled it to the surface. The stench of rotting vegetation made my stomach churn.

"Dan! Dan!" Although I was terrified, I plodded on. I moved slower now, because my feet were caked with muck and slime. I walked until I thought I could no longer drag one foot ahead of the other, then all at once the fog thinned. I saw the square stone house not twenty yards ahead of me.

"Hello! Hello!" I dashed to the door. This

was safe ground. No one would have a bog in his front yard. My footsteps on a flagged terrace alerted a dog inside the house. As it began to bark, an old wisp of a woman opened the door.

"Who's there?" she called.

I only caught a glimpse of birdlike arms and legs before she drew back, shielding her face with her hands.

"It's a ghost. Milord! A ghost!" She fainted.

"Emma! Emma!" A balding rotund man rushed to the woman's rescue. He fanned her with his handkerchief, and at the same time he tried to see me.

"I'm sorry, sir." I felt myself blushing. In the light that streamed through the doorway I could see the muck on my legs and arms and clothing. No wonder the lady had fainted.

"Who is it?" a robust voice called out, and then a blond young man invited me in. For a moment we stood staring at each other.

"I'm Margo Landon," I said. "A guest of Sir Henry Merton." I glanced through the doorway at a kitchen-sitting room. The young man stepped aside as his father moved forward.

"Come in." The older man, having revived his wife, pulled a straight chair up to the fire blazing on the hearth. "Welcome to Lanrith House."

"But I'll track up your floor."

The young man spoke. "People who live on the moor are used to a bit of mud. I'm Charles Lanrith. Let me take your shoes and clean them for you."

Slipping from the one shoe I still wore, I handed them both over, then followed the older man to the chair by the fire.

"A friend of Sir Henry's?" Mr. Lanrith asked. "The old gentlemen has few guests. You must be someone special."

"A ghost. That's what she is." Mrs. Lanrith's Gorgonian stare announced her open hostility.

"Tut, tut, Emma." Mr. Lanrith shot his wife with a sharp glance. "There's a resemblance, but this child's much younger. Why don't you brew some tea? The girl's shivering." Then turning to me, he asked, "What are you doing about on a night like this?"

"Dan Taledon from Merton Manor called for me in the village. His car skidded into a bog and he walked for help. When he didn't return, I decided to search for him."

"We have not seen him," Mrs. Lanrith called from the stove.

"Could you call the manor and ask if he

arrived safely?" I suggested.

"We have no call box," Mr. Lanrith replied. "But Charles can saddle Blaze and ride to the manor. That would be best."

"I can't ask you to do that. Not on a night like this."

"Miss, every night is a night like this." Mr. Lanrith smiled. "Blaze knows the trail. Horses are smarter than cars."

At that moment Charles returned with my shoes, which he had cleaned. Blushing furiously, I thanked him and slipped them on.

"I'll saddle Blaze and be back soon." Charles left the house, and a chill breeze blew in through the open door.

"Try a spot of tea, miss." Mrs. Lanrith stepped over a sheep dog who had plopped himself in front of the fireplace.

"Thank you, Mrs. Lanrith. It smells delicious." I hadn't realized how badly I needed the hot drink. Turning the cup so that the chipped rim wouldn't cut my lips, I took a sip of tea.

"Who are you, anyway?" Mrs. Lanrith asked.

"I'm Margo Landon. Sir Henry's granddaughter."

"Wanda's child!" Mrs. Lanrith exclaimed. "Is your mother with you? Tis years since we have seen her."

"My mother's dead." I spoke as calmly as if I were talking of a stranger. Why hadn't the Lanriths known?

"It is sad news you bring." Mr. Lanrith stretched his slippered feet toward the fire. "Sir Henry had not told us. But now you have come to live at the manor?"

"I'm only here for a visit," I replied.

Mr. Lanrith rubbed a work-worn hand over his bald head. "You are much like your aunt Angela."

"Aunt Angela." I repeated the words. "Dan's wife. She must have been Mother's younger sister." My teacup shook as I realized that it was my resemblance to Angela that had made Dan grow pale and that had frightened Mrs. Lanrith.

"Tis Muldoon you hear mourning, Angela's wolfhound." Mrs. Lanrith sighed. "He misses her. For over five years he has remembered. And who wouldn't remember a beauty as she!"

Mr. Lanrith shook his head. "The world's a darker place without Angela Merton. What a lively one she was. Rode her stallion like the devil himself was chasing her. She'd arrive here all flushed with a parcel of cookies or a special cake."

"Angela brightened the whole moor with her laughter and her winsome ways," Mrs.

Lanrith said. "Many folk criticized her, and the papers were cruel to her. But Angela was always kind to us, and we liked her. We ignored the gossip, and there was a lot of it. It was enough to make her take her own life. But her death was an accident — a catastrophe we never speak of."

"I think Angela was always Sir Henry's favorite," Mr. Lanrith said. "He's never been quite the same since her death, not quite reasonable."

"I admire my aunt Katherine's writing," I said, changing the subject. "I am quite eager to meet her."

"You're just in time for the party," Mrs. Lanrith said. "Each year Katherine throws a big party. There's music and food and dancing and hundreds of guests from all over England. The mister and I always help with the fixin's."

"What is your occupation, sir?" I asked Mr. Lanrith.

"Charles and I work the moors for Sir Henry. All this land belongs to the Mertons. We raise sheep, and we harvest some wheat and barley. It's nothing big, but it's a good life."

Before I could say anything, Charles flung the door open and blustered inside with a stranger following at his heels.

"Margo Landon, meet your uncle, Guilford Pease."

Everyone stood, and in the bustle I studied the man whom I guessed to be Sir Henry's foster son. I studied Guilford, and smelled him. He reeked of turpentine. Guilford was big, but not robust, and his patched jeans and paint-spattered turtle-neck sweater did little for him. A lock of hair falling over his forehead might have given his plain, craggy face a boyish look had it not seemed so hard and shell-like.

"Welcome to Cornwall." As Guilford shook my hand I noticed his slim, smooth fingers, yet his grip had a rock-hard mascu-linity about it. He studied my face as if he were trying to memorize it, and although he had a ready smile, his hazel eyes held a look of sadness that was accented by smudges of dark lashes.

"It was quite a welcome," I said, trying for a light touch. "What about Dan? Is he all right? Have you seen him?"

"He's fine." Guilford's voice rang deep and resonant. "He was lost on the moor and he's tired from the ordeal, but he'll be fit again in the morning."

Talk seemed to come easily to Guilford, and he helped smooth our leave-taking. He helped me into a white MG that he had parked near the house. I thought he would seem out of place in such a car, but its sleek lines and bucket seats suited him perfectly. He was a contradiction in plainness and sophistication.

On the ride to the manor Guilford chatted about anything and everything, and it was all I could do to get a word in.

"What about the car?" I asked. "Dan's car."

"We'll get it tomorrow in the daylight."

We were on a winding lane, and just for a moment when the fog thinned, I caught a glimpse of the manor. It loomed like a castle with projections and turrets jutting from its massive walls. The howling became unbearably loud as we approached the front entrance, where a massive double door stood slightly ajar.

"A greeting from Muldoon." Guilford nodded toward a huge Irish wolfhound that came running as we approached. The creature was almost as large as a pony, and its brownish coat stood in damp spikes. It would have been a formidable sight even if its muzzle hadn't been aimed at the sky in a blood-chilling howl.

"Angela's dog," I said.

"How did you know?"

"The Lanriths told me."

"Damn them. I suppose they filled your head with all sorts of nonsense." Guilford scowled.

"Well, it is Angela's dog, isn't it?"

"It was Angela's dog. It's my dog now."

"Then why don't you quiet him? That howling is almost too much to bear."

"I don't quiet him because I can't catch him." The sadness disappeared from Guilford's eyes, and they flashed fire.

His reply had a directness that I liked. Maybe we would get on all right when we became better acquainted. I couldn't expect a person who had been called out onto a foggy moor in the middle of the night to greet an uninvited guest to be jolly.

Guilford opened the car door for me, but I hesitated.

"Don't be afraid." He took my hand and helped me from the bucket seat. "Muldoon's harmless."

His words were true. As we approached the flagged terrace and the oaken doors, Muldoon ran into the night.

"Good riddance," I said.

Guilford watched Muldoon for a moment, then opened the heavy carved doors of the manor. "Come on inside, Margo." Guiding me by the elbow, Guilford ushered me into a cavernous,

36

dimly lighted hallway. A cold draft chilled my shoulders, and several moments passed before I noticed the woman standing at the top of the curving stairway.

CHAPTER FOUR

Although the woman on the stairway wore an ugly spinach-colored uniform and brown oxfords, she held her head high and approached us slowly, deliberately, like an actress performing the staircase scene in a romantic movie. If she was hoping to impress Guilford, she failed.

"Let me take your coat." Guilford ignored the woman.

"Please, I'll keep it on. My clothes are a mess."

We stood in a wide hallway. Doors opened on each side, but they were closed now and I could see little. The hall and stairway were heavy with faded maroon carpeting, and the polished spindles on the stairway gleamed in the dim light from a crystal chandelier. The manor smelled musty. Even the people in the gilt-framed portraits on the walls looked as if they needed a whiff of fresh air.

"Margo," Guilford said when the woman reached us at last, "I'd like you to meet Mrs. Foster. She's been with the family for years, and she's pretty much in charge here. She'll show you to your room and fetch anything you might need."

"I'm glad to know you, Mrs. Foster." I don't know why I took an immediate dislike to the woman. Vinegar Face. The nickname flashed unbidden into my mind. Her face was deeply wrinkled, and her hostile eyes scrutinized me from deep pouches of loose flesh. The Mertons could not have chosen a more appropriate person to frighten off their unwanted guest.

"Miss Landon has had an unfortunate experience." Guilford nodded at my ruined outfit. "Please do what you can for her clothing after you show her to her room. And loan her some night things. Her bags are in Dan's car."

I could feel Guilford's gaze following me as I trailed Vinegar Face up the curving staircase, but I did not turn. I sensed that he knew I was frightened, and I felt all the more vulnerable. An eerie atmosphere pervaded this huge manor. Or perhaps it was just in my mind. Any strange house seems spooky when it is only dimly lighted at night. I shuddered.

Vinegar Face abandoned her stately posing and moved with a speed that told me she was impatient to leave my presence. I almost had to trot to keep up with her.

Halfway up the steps I saw a small doorway that opened onto a narrow landing.

"Back stairway?" I asked.

Vinegar Face nodded, but didn't speak. At the top of the steps a long corridor stretched on either side of the stairway. I couldn't begin to count the doorways that opened onto the corridor, but I knew that there were a vast number of rooms on this upper floor of the manor. At one end of the corridor another flight of steps led to a third floor. Servants' quarters?

Leading me to a doorway about halfway down the corridor to our right, Vinegar Face said, "This will be your suite. It used to belong to your mother." She preceded me into an apartment of two rooms with a fireplace and a small bath.

"Mother's rooms!" I blinked back tears, determined not to let Mrs. Foster notice any sign of weakness on my part.

"This first room is your sitting room," Vinegar Face said. "At one time it was elegant in its appointments."

"It's still lovely." I touched the worn pink velvet of an easy chair and ottoman that filled one corner, and I admired a French Provincial couch done in gold needlepoint that dominated the side of the room near the door.

"That walnut desk and the brass lamp are beautiful. I'll enjoy it here." My toe caught on a worn place in the carpet, and I tripped as I walked toward the second room.

"This is your bedroom," Vinegar Face said. "I've laid out a nightgown, robe, and a pair of slippers."

I touched the silk of the canopied bed. Had the night things belonged to my mother?

"Is everything in order, Miss Landon?"

I nodded and smiled. "Please call me Margo. Everything's fine, and I do appreciate your thoughtfulness." I had to raise my voice to make it heard above the howling of the dog, which seemed to have taken up quarters directly under my window.

Holding a bony finger to her thin lips, Vinegar Face impatiently motioned me to silence. "Everyone's asleep at this hour. Katherine will be upset if she's disturbed."

"But how does anyone sleep with Muldoon howling so?"

"Miss Katherine is under sedation. Sir Henry turns his hearing aid off, and Dan and Guilford don't seem to let it bother them. Of course, the child can sleep through anything. It's Tillie and I who suffer." Mrs. Foster scowled.

"Child? Whose child?"

"Katherine's daughter. She has custody, you know." Mrs. Foster smoothed the knot of hair at her neckline and unconsciously tapped her toe. "Kimi sleeps through anything. If there's nothing more you need, I'll be going."

As soon as Vinegar Face was gone I checked the latch on the sitting-room door and secured the lock. I should not have been afraid in my mother's childhood rooms or in my grandfather's home, but I was. The rooms had a musty, closed-for-a-longtime odor, yet underlying that was the clinging fragrance of lavender, which used to be Mother's favorite scent.

I prepared for bed quietly, but when I kicked off my shoes, one of them struck a hard object beneath the bed.

Dropping to my knees, I groped on the carpeting until I pulled out my shoe and a sturdy wooden box that it had hit.

I shuddered. But my curiosity was stronger than my fear. I raised the lid from the box and stared at a thick, snakelike coil of rope. A fire rope. That was all.

It was only when I curled under the covers that I felt the draft blowing across my head. Dank and damp, it carried the smell and taste of salt air. Rising, I snapped on my bedside lamp.

I pulled the light silk draperies aside and found that the middle of three windows was wide open. There was no screen. I reached out and touched the night.

Had Vinegar Face left this window open deliberately to foster my discomfort? Before I closed it, I stood for a moment in the dark, listening to the pounding of the surf and touching the locket that hung around my neck.

Although I was sure I wouldn't sleep a wink in the eerie manor surrounded by sea sounds, the sun streaming on my pillow awakened me the next morning. I had forgotten to close the drapery. For a moment I couldn't remember where I was as I stared at the lacy pink canopy over my head. Then the faint odor of lavender reminded me of my mother and of Merton Manor.

A sharp rap on my door brought me from my bed.

"Who's there?" I slipped into the robe and opened the door. Vinegar Face was waiting in the corridor with my luggage.

"How nice!" I exclaimed. "But how did it get here?"

"Mr. Dan fetched it with Mr. Guilford's help, of course." Vinegar Face pinched her features into what passed for a smile.

"Breakfast's served in a few minutes,

43

ma'am. Everyone is eager to meet you. I'll wait and show you to the dining room."

"Come in." I stepped aside to let Vinegar Face enter my sitting room. "If you'll excuse me, I'll get dressed." I went into the bedroom, closing the door between the rooms.

"Do hurry, Miss Landon," Vinegar Face called.

Shaking the wrinkles from a jumper and a blouse, I dressed quickly and rejoined her.

This morning as Mrs. Foster led the way downstairs I almost had to run to keep up. Clearly, her dramatic descent of the night before had been for show. For Guilford?

A hush fell over the dining room as we entered. "Good morning," I said.

Guilford and Dan rose from their places at an oval-shaped table. Then, as they were seated once more, Guilford performed the introductions.

"Margo, this is your aunt Katherine." Guilford nodded to the woman sitting at his right, who was smoking the last tip end of a cigarette she held in a sleek black holder.

"It's good to know you, Aunt Katherine." The words rang strange in my ears. Why had this woman withheld my letters from my grandfather? I felt myself blushing under Katherine Merton's appraising gaze. Then I

44

realized that she was gazing more at my throat than at my face. Instinctively I reached to touch my mother's locket. I buttoned the top button of my blouse, hiding the locket from view. From Katherine's haughty air I guessed that she had never been called Kate in her whole life.

"Your dust-jacket photos don't do you justice, Aunt Katherine."

"I trust that is a compliment," Katherine replied.

Katherine reminded me of a Siamese cat. Her hair was the color of black olives, and her eyes were ice-blue and set in a pale, triangular face. She didn't blend in with the homey odor of bacon and eggs that filled the room.

"Katherine, is she my new cousin?" Kimi looked at her mother, and I was surprised to hear the child call Katherine by her first name. There was coldness in the sound.

"That's right, Kimi," Guilford answered for Katherine. "Margo's your cousin. Margo, meet Kimi. She's been counting the minutes until you came to the table."

"Hello, Kimi." I slipped into the chair Vinegar Face guided me toward, and I knew immediately that Kimi was my friend. "I hope you'll show me around Merton Manor after we have breakfast. Do you have time?"

"Oh, may I, Katherine? May I?" Kimi's blue eyes implored her mother, who nodded her consent as she slipped a wrinkled paper napkin from under her place mat and spread it on her lap.

Guilford placed both hands gently on Kimi's shoulders, shushing her while he introduced me to my grandfather.

"Margo, this is Sir Henry."

Sir Henry and I stared at each other. He was the man in my nightmares. I felt terror like a tight band around my throat. Sir Henry sat in a captain's chair at the table's oval curve, but somehow I sensed that wherever Katherine sat was the head of the table. Even though Sir Henry was seated, I could tell that he was still tall and slender. He had a full head of silvery hair, but even Dan's description and my nightmares hadn't prepared me for the coal-black eyebrows.

Sir Henry rested his right hand on an ornately carved walnut cane. He reminded me of a majestic eagle as tough and craggy as these Cornish cliffs where he had spent a lifetime.

"Grandfather, I'm glad to know you." Somehow I blurted the words, determined to separate dreams from reality. I was surprised when Sir Henry scowled.

"You needn't try to deceive me, Angela. And the rest of you! Do you take me for a fool? An idiot who doesn't know his own child! Angela! Where have you been?"

Mr. Lanrith's words of the night before rang in my ears: *"He's never been quite the same since her death, not quite reasonable."*

At that moment a plump, red-faced girl entered the dining room from the kitchen. She carried a silver tray with one crystal glass in the center. Moving slowly, she let her stomach lead the way, and the rest of her seemed in no hurry to follow.

"Your cranberry juice, sir." She plopped the glass in front of Sir Henry and bowed.

"Thank you, Tillie," Sir Henry said. "At least one of my household still respects my wishes."

No one spoke as Sir Henry sipped his juice. My own mouth puckered at the thought of cranberry juice for breakfast, but my grandfather seemed to enjoy it. When he emptied the glass and set it aside, he looked directly at me.

"You must be Margo, my granddaughter. Why hasn't someone introduced us?"

"I was just getting ready to do that." Guilford smiled and repeated the introduction.

This time I was able to respond at once.

"Good morning, Grandfather. It is wonderful to be here with you."

Sir Henry Merton may have haunted my dreams, but now my fear diminished. He was a sick man; my sympathy went out to him.

Tillie and Vinegar Face served a delicious breakfast, and everyone chatted agreeably — everyone except Dan. He had nothing to say. For the first time since my arrival I was glad I had come to Merton Manor. I would give Mother's locket to Sir Henry at the earliest opportunity and free myself from the nightmares that had haunted me. Surely there was no danger here.

"What a beautiful home you have, Sir Henry! It's like an ancient castle. I can hardly believe it's real."

"It was a gift to one of my ancestors from King Henry the Second," Sir Henry said, breaking a piece of toast into bits and slipping it into the pocket of his jacket. "Lucky bloke."

"The king?" I asked.

"No. My ancient relative." Sir Henry laughed and pounded his cane on the floor. "The story of the gift is almost a legend. I intend to include it in my next book. I'm working on a volume of Cornish legends, you know. It'll never be a bestseller like

Katherine's novels are, but it will contain information that should be recorded for posterity."

"Tell us the legend." Kimi smiled. "I like your stories."

Sir Henry patted Kimi on the head, and the rest of the family began to squirm. I guessed that they had heard the story before. As Sir Henry began to speak, Vinegar Face passed Guilford more toast and offered him the platter of eggs and bacon.

"Back in the far distant past murder by poison was a common occurrence," Sir Henry began. "Every king feared for his life. As a precaution King Henry the Second appointed a food taster. This man's job was to taste each dish before the king ate it."

"If the taster didn't become ill, then the king ate. Right?" I asked.

"Correct." Sir Henry smiled. "A food taster possessed much courage. Archibald Merton was my ancestor on my mother's side of the family. The Merton name came from both sides, you see. He served his king faithfully, and as a reward for years of service, the king gave him this manor. We Mertons have been Cornishmen ever since."

By the time Sir Henry ended his tale everyone had finished eating. But he spoke again.

"That tale reminds me of another . . ."

"We've had quite enough for one morning," Katherine interrupted her father. "Let's be about the day's work."

Sir Henry reluctantly excused the family from the table. I hated to see the meal end. I had enjoyed Sir Henry's tale, but he had dominated the conversation. I wanted to know Aunt Katherine. Of course I knew it was far too soon to approach the subject of a professional interview. But I wanted to hear her talk and thus reveal facets of her personality.

"I get to show Margo around," Kimi announced to Sir Henry. "Katherine said so. She really did." Kimi seemed to be the only member of the household who could speak freely to Sir Henry.

"Let's do it together," Sir Henry suggested. "The three of us will make a morning excursion of the estate."

I had hoped to be able to give Mother's locket to Sir Henry, but I wanted to do it privately. I would wait until a time when Kimi was absent.

"Come on, Margo." Kimi tugged at my hand, then seeing that I was going to match my pace to Sir Henry's, she let me go and danced on outside ahead of us.

"Merton Manor is magnificent," I said to Sir Henry. "It's far too grand to take in at a glance."

"It's stones are weather-beaten, but as a fortress it has warded off all attack except the assault of the sea. The salt wind stunts the trees." Sir Henry pointed to the pines that grew at the corner of the manor. "It even stunts the grass that tries to grow between the flags of the terrace."

"Let's go see the horses," Kimi shouted.

"Shall we humor her?" Sir Henry asked.

"Let's do." I saw part of a frame structure rising behind a thicket of brambles, and we headed toward it.

When we reached the stable, Sir Henry pushed the door open with the tip of his cane. I squinted into the darkness until he lighted an oil lamp and hung it from an overhead beam. The sweet odor of hay mingled with the stench of horse manure, and a mare and a stallion whinnied at our approach.

"A sorrel and a bay!" I exclaimed. Although their manes and tails were well groomed, they were still shedding their winter coats and had a fuzzy look. "Who tends them?"

"Dan does. Angela used to ride the stallion, Diablo. She was the only one who could handle him. But he's older now; sometimes Dan saddles him for a run."

I patted the horses, but Kimi was already dashing from the stable. She was like a grasshopper, flitting from one place to another almost quicker than the eye could follow. Outside the stable I stood on the clifftop and gazed a hundred feet or more straight down to the beach, where the tide creamed around dark boulders. I started to follow the clifftop path back toward the manor, and I had taken several steps before I realized that Sir Henry wasn't following. Kimi came and grabbed my hand.

"We never walk that way." Kimi led me back to where Sir Henry was poking in a hollow stump with the tip of his cane.

"My pet toads live here," he said. "See?" He raised dead leaves and twigs with the cane, and I saw two toads crouched at the bottom of the stump.

"Kwee-kwii. Kwii-kwee." Sir Henry spoke the strange words in a high singsong voice, then cocked his head to listen.

"They're asking for their breakfast. Do you hear them, Angela?" Sir Henry reached into his jacket pocket and pulled out his breakfast toast. As he bent over the stump to feed the toads, Kimi whispered in my ear.

"I don't hear the toads talking, but sometimes I pretend that I do. It pleases Grandfather."

I didn't know whether to smile or cry. Sometimes Sir Henry was completely rational, but at other times he was more childish than Kimi. I couldn't give him the locket until I was sure he knew I was Margo, Wanda's daughter.

As he finished feeding the toads, I glanced toward the manor and saw Katherine watching us from an upstairs window. Her gaze sent a chill over me, and I buttoned my sweater. When I glanced at the window again, Katherine was gone. But I knew she had been watching.

CHAPTER FIVE

Sir Henry's moods puzzled and dismayed me. It was disconcerting to be called Angela; I never knew how to react. As we strolled back toward the manor, I saw Mr. and Mrs. Lanrith working on the grounds. Mr. Lanrith's head gleamed in the sunlight as he pulled weeds. Mrs. Lanrith carried a pail of water and was preparing to wash windows.

"They're getting ready for Katherine's party." Kimi danced to where the Lanriths were working. I followed.

"It's good to see you again," I said. "The world seems brighter today than it did last night. I want to thank you once more for your hospitality."

"Aye, and you are welcome, that you are." Mr. Lanrith spoke to me, then bowed to Sir Henry.

"Angela's home," Sir Henry said. "It's good to have her back. It's like old times again."

The Lanriths said nothing, and on the pretext of following Kimi, I hurried Sir Henry on into the house.

Vinegar Face was waiting inside the door

with tapping toe, and before we could exchange greetings, she whisked Sir Henry off for his morning rest. I suddenly felt very sorry for my grandfather. At breakfast I had seen him bow to Katherine's wishes, and now he followed Mrs. Foster like an obedient spaniel.

"Would you like to tour the house?"

I hadn't heard Aunt Katherine approach, and I jumped, startled. She wore bright blue rope-soled sandals that muted her footsteps, and she held the butt of a cigarette in an ebony holder in one hand and a sketch in the other. As she crossed the worn carpeting she flicked off a light switch.

"I'd love to see it," I said, "but I don't want to keep you from your writing. I could just as well busy myself writing a note to my cousin. I intended to do that first thing, but I've misplaced my pen."

"Oh, this week's the party. A big deal." Katherine gestured with her cigarette holder. "The Lanriths, Tillie, Mrs. Foster, Charles, and even Dan and Guilford pitch in to make it a success. I don't try to write with such an uproar going on around me, but usually I do spend the day at my typewriter." Katherine's voice trailed off, and she changed the subject.

"See my dress." Katherine held the

sketch toward me. "Guilford designed it, and a Paris house is making it up for me."

I studied the sketch and admired Guilford's talent. The low-cut bodice would accent Katherine's figure, and the pencil-slim skirt with its side slits would show off her well-formed legs.

"It suits you perfectly," I said. "Is it for your birthday? The dress and the party, I mean?"

Katherine purred laughter. "My dear, I quit celebrating birthdays ages ago. But each year after my latest book comes out I invite England's literary world to the manor. At the end of the week you'll meet editors, publishers, critics — the whole bit."

As Katherine stopped speaking a snarl broke the silence, and Muldoon rushed at her with bared teeth. Katherine screamed and leaped upon a chair, and in a reflex motion I grabbed the dog's collar. He was about to break from my grip when Guilford appeared and took charge, leading the wolf-hound toward the kitchen.

I was trembling as Katherine climbed down from her perch.

"Is he dangerous?" I asked.

"Muldoon and I have never been close friends." Katherine snorted. "But he's usually outdoors or confined to the kitchen."

"Why did you keep my letters from Sir Henry?" I shot the question while Katherine was still unnerved over Muldoon's attack.

Katherine showed no discomposure. "I didn't want to disturb a sick man."

"But even the others didn't know I was coming."

"I tried to avoid a family ruckus with everyone taking sides and all. Why did you come?"

"I came to meet my mother's family." I decided to keep the locket a secret. I vowed that Katherine would know the real reason for my visit only if Sir Henry cared to tell her.

Katherine opened huge double doors that led into the sitting room of the manor. Three crystal chandeliers dangled from the ceiling. Katherine turned only one of them on. Light hitting the prisms shot rainbows of color over the room.

Worn Oriental carpets decorated the floors, and from four walls Katherine Merton overlooked the scene from life-size, gold-framed portraits. Then there were other pictures. Katherine autographing books. Katherine boarding a jet. Katherine smiling graciously in a reception line. Katherine. Katherine. Katherine.

The drawing room was furnished with the

curves and swirls of some bygone French era, and everywhere there were copies of Katherine's books. One wall held a floor-to-ceiling hanging of French brocade that was embossed with dust jackets.

"I've seen all those before, Aunt Katherine. I'm such a Katherine Merton fan I can recite the jacket blurbs from memory."

"I've moved the family portraits into the alcove." Katherine led the way to a smaller room that jutted off from the main room. "I thought you might want to see Angela's picture." Katherine tilted her tiny catlike face at an appraising angle and studied my every feature. "You do resemble her, you know."

"So I've been told." If Katherine was trying to shake me up, she was in for disappointment. It would take more than looking at a portrait to unnerve me. But how silly! Katherine was only being hospitable. It was only natural of her to assume that I would be interested in Angela's portrait.

The alcove wall was a mass of pictures, but it didn't take me long to spot Angela.

"Oh!" I stifled a gasp. No wonder Mrs. Lanrith had screamed. No wonder Dan had turned pale. I felt as if I were staring at a likeness of myself. Reaching up, I snapped on the small light meant to illumine the portrait.

Mrs. Lanrith had said that Angela had been beautiful, but that wasn't true. She looked like me. Perhaps her personality had created an illusion of beauty, but besides blue eyes and a slim figure she had the same humped nose that I had inherited and the same pointed chin and tobacco-colored hair. I sighed.

"She wasn't really beautiful, was she?" I kept staring at the portrait, hoping to see the beauty Mrs. Lanrith saw.

"No. I never thought she was." Katherine snapped off the light almost before I had finished looking at the portrait.

"Lunch is served," Vinegar Face called to us, and we went to the dining room. I was glad to escape the alcove.

We all took the same places we had occupied at breakfast. Dan popped a Pepto disk into his mouth as Tillie appeared with a steaming tureen.

"Stew and biscuits," Tillie announced, serving Sir Henry first. Kimi prattled on about the horses and the toads as Tillie served us, and I studied Dan and Guilford.

Dan was as handsome as Guilford was plain and as silent as Guilford was talkative. Guilford joined in conversation with Kimi as if there were no generation gap, but Dan sat in brooding silence chewing his Pepto. I wished he would say more. Speech reveals character, and I wanted to know Dan better.

"I've been showing Margo around the house," Katherine said when Kimi ran out of talk.

"It's lovely," I added. "We only had time to do the downstairs, but it's charming."

"Katherine has made it hers." Guilford spoke with more dryness than I thought necessary. Was he jealous?

I felt drawn to Katherine in spite of her coolness. When I was in high school, I had written a poem that appeared in the local newspaper. Mother had framed it and hung it on my bedroom wall. Nothing had ever pleased me quite so much. I understood Katherine.

As Mrs. Foster refilled Guilford's coffee cup, which he had barely touched, Guilford laid a swatch of fabric on the arm of his chair.

"What is that?" I asked. "Surely you're not going to reupholster the furniture before the party!"

Guilford darted Katherine a quick look. "No. Nothing as rash as all that." He handed me the fabric. "I have a client in Exeter who wants her walls papered in this fabric."

"Someone told me you were an artist. I thought you painted for a living."

"He does paint," Kimi piped up. "He paints pictures for me, don't you, Uncle Gil?"

"I'm an artist by inclination and love, and an interior decorator by profession." Guilford pulled his muscles into a half smile. "I've been with Antwerp and Dugan for the past ten years."

"You commute to your office from here?"

"Yes." Guilford stuffed the cloth back into his pocket. "But the company has offices in all large cities, and my work often involves visiting clients in their homes. Sometimes I'm away for a few days at a time, but it works out. I like it here. Of course, when I have my own business . . ."

Turning to me, Katherine said, "Margo, tell us about your life in America. What do you do? Where do you live?"

"I live in a small ranch-style house in a suburb of New York, and I've spent most of my life going to school. High school, college, then I landed a reading job in a publishing house."

"The Mertons always have been a literary family." Pride filled Sir Henry's voice. "Do you write?"

"I try." Suddenly I felt shy at mentioning

61

my writing ambitions. But I couldn't resist the chance to query my aunt.

"Aunt Katherine, I've been wondering if you would grant me an interview before I leave Merton Manor. I know that you don't usually do this, but my position at the publishing house would be greatly enhanced if I returned with a small article about the famous Katherine Merton."

I was sorry immediately. Everyone at the table looked away from Katherine and me — everyone except Dan, whose gaze bored into Katherine's face with an intensity I found embarrassing.

"Too bad." Katherine laughed, but her eyes flashed fire. "Keeping my private life a mystery is my stock in trade. People are always curious about the unknown. Once their curiosity is satisfied, their interest diminishes. I'm sure you'll understand. An interview would be bad for my career."

"Of course," I said. "I understand."

Kimi relieved the tension by scooting from her chair. "Grandfather, come. It's time to feed the toads."

"And then it's time for your nap," Vinegar Face said. "I'll give you ten minutes outside, no more."

Kimi and Sir Henry left the room, but the rest of us were still lingering at the table when they returned. Sir Henry went upstairs to his suite, but Kimi refused to follow Vinegar Face to her room.

"Won't go!" she screamed. "Won't! Won't!"

Vinegar Face jerked her by one arm, and Kimi pulled back, kicking and screaming. I gasped. I didn't blamed Kimi for her tantrum. It didn't surprise me that Vinegar Face inspired that sort of thing.

Katherine blew smoke rings toward the ceiling, and when Guilford rose to go to his niece, she spoke sharply.

"You'll spoil her, Gil. Leave the child alone. Mrs. Foster can manage."

But Vinegar Face couldn't manage. Kimi kicked the housekeeper, jerked free of her grasp, and ran straight to me.

"Margo! Margo will take me to my room. Won't you, Margo?"

"No." Katherine stubbed out her cigarette, but Guilford spoke in a tone so firm that there was no arguing with him.

"If Margo doesn't mind, I'm sure it will do no harm. Mrs. Foster, you help Tillie in the kitchen."

"I don't mind at all," I said. "I was going upstairs to write to my cousin anyway." I reached for Kimi's hand, which she offered willingly. "I'll tell you a story about America."

"There's a pen on my desk," Katherine said. "Help yourself, or use my typewriter if you care to."

Kimi went with me willingly, and I called a thank-you to Katherine. It was obvious to me that she was trying to smooth over her refusal to grant an interview.

At the top of the stairs Kimi pointed. "That room's mine. Katherine's is across the hall."

I was surprised to find Kimi's suite so similar to mine. For so young a child I had pictured a nursery. After a long story Kimi sat up in her bed and stared out her window at the ocean. I prepared to leave the room without insisting that she lie down. She had been so disturbed by Vinegar Face that I knew she needed to unwind at her own rate of speed.

Calling after me, Kimi asked, "In America do people pinch?"

"What do you mean?"

Kimi pushed up her sleeve and showed me a red welt on her arm. "Mrs. Foster pinches me. Do people pinch in America?"

"Perhaps Mrs. Foster didn't mean to pinch you," I said, doubting my words. "You were ugly to her, you know."

"But I'm nice to you," Kimi said. "We're friends. Tell me another story."

Before I had half finished my second tale, Kimi fell asleep. I slipped from her room. This upper corridor with its row of closed doors fascinated me. I didn't want to pry, but I was curious as to which suite belonged to whom. From behind one door I could hear Sir Henry snoring, and I found another door open. Peeking inside, I decided that that suite was unoccupied. Perhaps it was another guest suite.

I went to my own rooms for notepaper. Had someone been here? I studied the suite. Had I left my suitcase so rumpled? No, surely I hadn't. I had the decided impression that someone had gone through my belongings. But I wasn't sure. And what would anyone be hunting for?

I hurried to Katherine's sitting room. I felt rather like an intruder even though Katherine had given me permission to enter. Portraits of Katherine were everywhere, and the bookshelf held only her books.

The typewriter was on Katherine's desk, and I hurriedly typed a note to Julia. The type on the machine looked like script, and I thought of my former employer and how he hated to receive manuscripts that had been typed on such a machine. But Katherine was so famous that she could use any sort of typewriter she cared to.

I finished my note and hurried back downstairs.

"Please let me help you with the party preparations," I said to Mrs. Foster. "Tell me what you'd like done."

"Oh, but you are a guest." She shook her head reprovingly, making me feel as if I had blundered by offering my help.

I wandered to the kitchen, where Tillie was still bustling about. She glanced up in surprise, then her work-roughened hands flew to her ears and she snatched off a pair of jeweled earrings and dropped them into her apron pocket.

"Don't take them off, Tillie. They're beautiful."

"Thank ye, ma'am, but they were a gift, and I promised not to wear them here at work. It's a hard promise to keep, for work is almost all I ever do."

I smiled to myself, wondering what Tillie's boyfriend was like. How often did she get to see him and to wear her jewelry? But I didn't ask. I didn't want to pry.

"What excellent biscuits you bake, Tillie. Is your recipe a secret?"

Tillie burst into a smile, her face as mobile as a rubber mask. "Ye liked them, Miss Margo?"

"I certainly did, Tillie. I like to cook. It's sort of a hobby."

I hadn't seen the wolfhound sleeping on the flagstone floor until Tillie nudged him from her way. I jumped back in fright, remembering how he had lunged at Katherine. But now Muldoon wagged his tail in friendly greeting.

"Well, glory be!" Tillie exclaimed. "Muldoon likes the looks of ye."

"I'm thrilled," I said, trying to compose myself.

"Ye should be honored, miss." Tillie lifted her recipe file from a shelf, picked out the card with the biscuit recipe, and gave it to me with a blank card and a pencil.

"Muldoon's particular who he befriends. Mr. Guilford and meself can usually manage him, but he hates Foster and Miss Katherine. He used to be *her* dog, ye know. Probably likes ye because ye look so much like her."

I began copying the recipe. When I finished my small chore, Tillie was busy rolling dough.

"What are you making now?" I asked her.

"Sweets for tea. We have high tea at five o'clock and dinner at nine."

"Oh." I wondered if I could adjust my gastric juices to an English schedule. "Do you ever make Spanish sugar cookies?"

Tillie shook her head. "Would ye want to show me how?" Then before I could reply, she answered her own question. "But of course ye wouldn't. Scullery work is for the likes of me, not for a fine lady like yourself."

"I'll help you." I started peering in cupboards. "I think I can remember the recipe."

Tillie and I measured ingredients, mixed batter, and baked the cookies, and when Kimi wakened from her nap, she joined us to sample the sweets. I felt that my time in the kitchen had won me another friend, perhaps two, if I counted Muldoon.

Later that afternoon only Katherine and Sir Henry and I had tea together, and I was glad when it ended and I was free to go to my room. For some reason I felt ill at ease around my aunt. At any rate, I welcomed a nap.

When I awakened, my room was dark. Fog had moved in, blanketing the moor with its murky dampness. I glanced at my watch. Eight-forty-five. I hurried downstairs.

The whole family appeared for dinner, but Sir Henry refused to eat. Finally Vinegar Face led him from the room.

"But shouldn't he eat?" I asked. "He seems so frail."

"And no wonder," Katherine said. "He's always so busy telling legends at mealtimes that he has little time to eat."

I slipped from my chair, picked up my own plate, and then picked up Sir Henry's plate of untouched food.

"If you'll allow me, I'll go upstairs and try to persuade him to eat. I'm sure that having me here has excited him. Let me make amends. Perhaps the two of us can eat together."

Katherine's eyes glittered. She shook her head and opened her mouth to protest, but Guilford overruled her.

"Let her go, Katherine. Sir Henry needs a good meal."

When I entered Sir Henry's rooms, he was sitting propped up in his bed. I smelled the medicinal odor of camphor.

"Angela." He said the name softly. "So you've come. None of the rest of them care if I starve. But you've come. Sit here by me where I can see the light on your hair."

I sat down by my grandfather and fed him his supper. Sir Henry said little after he ate, and I doubted that he recognized me. Here we were alone, yet I couldn't give him the locket — not when his mind was confused.

When we both finished eating, I returned our plates to the kitchen and excused myself from the family for the evening.

Once alone in my room sleep eluded me. I tossed in bed, and when I finally dozed I was soon wakened by the horrible nightmare that had plagued me in New York. This time I didn't scream. And it was just as well, for there was nobody to comfort me. Again I tossed and rolled, unable to get to sleep.

Two hours later I was still wide awake. Midnight! Easing from bed, I slipped on my robe and slippers and stepped into the corridor.

Something attracted me to the empty rooms I had seen that afternoon. Tiptoeing down the hallway, I slipped through the open doorway into the empty suite.

The floor plan was the same as the one for my own rooms, so I turned on no lamps. The light from the corridor was sufficient. Walking from the sitting room into the bedroom, I pulled the draperies, raised the window, and peered into the night. The sound of the surf carried on the breeze, and the smell of salt and damp blew into the room. Feeling chilled, I closed the window and turned to leave the room.

Darkness enveloped me. No light shone

in from the corridor. The hairs along the back of my neck rose as I reached the sitting-room door and found it closed and locked.

CHAPTER SIX

The door's blown shut, I thought. There had been a draft when I raised the window. I groped in the dark, feeling for the spring lock. There was none. My fingers touched the polished wood of the door, and then I felt the cold metal of an ordinary lock, the sort that requires a key. There was no key.

With an outstretched hand in front of me I peered into the darkness and fumbled for the light switch. There! I felt its metal beneath my fingertips. I snapped it on. No light.

Lamps, I thought. There would be lamps with live bulbs in them. In my rising panic I crashed into an ottoman, making a thud that would surely rouse someone. I waited. Silence. My heart pounded, but I forced myself to inch carefully through the suite. I snapped the switch on every lamp. None of them worked. I couldn't bear the thought of being imprisoned all night.

I tapped on the wall. "Please," I called. "I've locked myself in. Help!"

I held my breath and listened. No answer. I tapped again.

"Please, do you hear me? I'm locked in."

Still no answer. Why, oh, why had I ever wandered into this trap! I was trembling, and when I heard the sniffing outside the door, I began to shake violently. Muldoon! I couldn't bear it if the creature started his doleful howling.

"Muldoon," I called through the door, speaking softly and gently, as if an Irish wolfhound could understand English. "Muldoon, go bring help. Help, Muldoon!"

"Muldoon likes the looks of ye." Tillie's words popped into my mind. Perhaps Muldoon would sound some sort of alarm. In a few moments he did just that. But it wasn't the sort of alarm I had in mind. He began the horrible keening that seemed to be his main stock in trade. The howling had seemed eerie outdoors, but indoors it sounded as if all the tortured souls in hell were wailing their woes in the hallway of Merton Manor. I pounded on the door with my fists.

Muldoon and I raised such a racket that I didn't know anyone was approaching until a key turned in the lock. The door creaked open. Muldoon stopped howling. I blinked into the dim light of the corridor, where the whole household had assembled. Eyes impaled me to the spot.

"Are you all right?" Holding Muldoon by the collar, Guilford stepped forward. Dan and Sir Henry remained in the background.

"Of course she's all right." Knotting the sash of her blue and beige robe, Katherine spoke up before I could reply. Muldoon growled and bared his teeth, but Guilford quieted him.

"What were you doing in that suite, Margo?" Katherine asked.

"Maybe Miss Margo sleepwalks," Tillie said.

Tillie was trying to help me save face; I smiled my thanks. For a moment she offered a bit of comic relief. She wore a crocheted nightcap and a short robe, and her knees and her bare feet were as apple-red as her cheeks. She looked like a sly troll as she stood by Vinegar Face, who for some reason was still fully dressed in her bilious green uniform.

"I'm sorry to have disturbed everyone," I said. "I couldn't sleep, so I just wandered into this empty suite for no special reason at all. The door was open — that is, it was open until I tried to return to my own quarters."

Katherine sighed and glanced at her wristwatch. Already Vinegar Face was urging Sir Henry back to his rooms, and

Dan had turned and was halfway down the corridor.

"I hope you'll be able to sleep now," Katherine said, ignoring Kimi, who was clutching at the skirt of her robe.

"I'm sure I will," I replied. "And I'm sorry for disturbing everyone. Really sorry."

With burning cheeks I escaped to my own quarters. I was still sitting up mulling over the frightening events when someone knocked lightly on my door.

Opening it a crack, I saw Guilford standing in the hallway.

"I guessed you'd still be up," he said. "You've had a devil of a fright. Come on downstairs. I'll pour you a brandy."

I never hesitated. I needed someone to talk to, and although I seldom drank, the thought of brandy drew me like a magnet. Guilford led me to the dining room and drew two chairs up before the fireplace. He lighted the fire that Tillie had laid, then brought out a decanter of apricot brandy and poured us each a glass.

The burning liquid seared my mouth and throat, but the drink and the fire warmed me.

"Someone must have been trying to frighten me," I said. "Katherine doesn't want me here, Guilford."

"Now, don't jump to conclusions." Guilford didn't smile.

"I'm not jumping to conclusions. She wrote to me, told me not to come here."

"Then why did you come?"

"I came to see my grandfather. When I've had a satisfactory visit with him, I'll leave. But I won't be frightened off."

"Why are you so sure someone was trying to frighten you?"

"What else am I to think? That door didn't close and lock itself."

"That was Angela's suite, you know." Guilford spoke in an ordinary voice, but his words hit my eardrums like stones.

"Angela's rooms! I should have known. Someone didn't want me in her suite."

"More than likely Dan locked the door," Guilford said. "He hates to see it open. I suppose it reminds him too much of Angela. Dan may have locked it, not knowing anyone was inside. Or perhaps Sir Henry locked it."

"Sir Henry? Why would my grandfather want to frighten me?"

"You know by now that his mind wanders." Guilford refilled our glasses. "And you do remind him of Angela. Sir Henry used to try to punish Angela by locking her in her room."

"*Tried* to punish her!" I exclaimed with a hollow laugh. "I should think he would have succeeded."

"That's because you never knew Angela." Guilford's lips curved into a sneering sort of smile. "A locked door meant nothing to her. She was a daredevil. She would merely use the fire rope and escape out her window."

"From the second story?"

"From the second story." Guilford swirled the brandy in his glass. "So you see, the door might have been locked in all innocence as far as you are concerned."

"I hope you're right. I know that Katherine doesn't really want me here. The knowledge makes me nervous, of course. But I have the feeling that Katherine wouldn't like any company at the manor unless it was her own idea."

"Katherine is used to having her own way about things." Guilford shrugged. "And you do rather complicate life for her."

"Why? I didn't know."

"It's simple. With Angela dead and with your mother both dead and disinherited, Katherine and I are in line to inherit the Merton fortune. And Sir Henry is an old, old man. With you here, Katherine sees the big pie being split three ways."

"I had no idea. I can hardly get used to the

fact that Sir Henry is really my grandfather. The thought of an inheritance had never entered my head. I've not come here for money, and surely Katherine Merton, the famous author, has more wealth than she knows what to do with."

"Your aunt Katherine never has enough of anything." Guilford snorted, but he didn't elaborate.

"Vinegar Face would like to see me leave," I said.

"Who?" Guilford asked.

I felt blood rush to my face. "I'm sorry. Mrs. Foster."

"Vinegar Face!" Guilford laughed until his eyes watered. "The most apropos nickname I've ever heard."

"I can feel her dislike and disapproval in everything she says and does," I said. "But I've no idea why. Of course I do make more work for her, the extra suite and all. And you know, Guilford, I believe Mrs. Foster's a bit in love with you."

"With me?" Guilford flushed. "Why do you say that?"

"Just my observations." I remembered the previous night and Vinegar Face's descent down the stairs. "Her eyes follow you wherever you go, whatever you do. At mealtimes you get the red-carpet treatment. I'm surprised you haven't grown fat from all the food she plies you with. Has she never married?"

"Not that I know of." Guilford stared into the crackling fire. "She's been with the family longer than I have, and I believe that her mother worked here before her."

"How did Angela die?" I was not used to drinking, and the brandy was making me bold. "I mean, of course, if you'd rather not speak of it . . ."

"It's certainly no secret." Guilford's slim smooth hands caressed the graceful brandy snifter, and as he looked down, studying his drink, his sooty eyelashes reminded me of dark smudges against his cheeks. The brandy and his easy manner made me feel as if I had known him forever.

"Angela loved the sunlight." Guilford looked directly at me. "Perhaps because there's so little of it here on these cliffs it seemed all the more precious to her. She loved to swim and to sunbathe. The sea seemed to draw her to it. Each day after she had squeezed the last ounce of sunlight from the sky, she would sit on a logan and watch the fog roll in."

"A logan? I don't understand."

"At several spots along this rugged coast there're what we call logans or rocking stones. They're flat slabs of rock that have been undercut by wind and rain until they wobble on a point of balance." Guilford rose and poked the fire until sparks flew and flames licked higher onto the logs.

"There used to be a logan stone on the cliff near the stables," Guilford continued. "Angela would sit there at tea time and stare out across the sea as if she were willing the fog to disperse. She would rock on the stone until it swayed back and forth. Then one day it happened. She pushed her luck one tilt too far. The logan became unbalanced. It gave way and crashed over the cliff. Angela was killed instantly."

"How horrible. How horrible for everyone."

I was sorry that I had saddened Guilford by making him repeat the unpleasant tale. But my curiosity was satisfied. Now I could understand the brooding look in Dan's eyes. My sympathy went out to him.

Somewhere in the depths of the manor a clock chimed, and I jumped with a start.

"Two o'clock, Guilford! I had no idea. I thank you so much for taking pity on me, but I must get back to my room. I didn't mean to keep you up all night."

"There's no rush — unless, of course, you're sleepy." Guilford stared into the fire.

"I rather enjoy being kept up. I find you very attractive, Margo. I hope you realize I'm your uncle in name only."

I flushed at Guilford's words. "I understand that you are Sir Henry's foster son. Who were your parents?" My voice took on the shrillness it gathers when I'm embarrassed.

"Fortunately for me, my mother was a cook here at the manor when I was a small child. She was a widow, and your grandmother took pity on her — kept her here long after illness left her unable to work. The story goes that on her deathbed my mother asked only one thing. She asked that your grandmother care for me. Your grandmother promised to do so, and she kept her word. She was a grand lady, Margo. She could have raised me as a servant, but instead she raised me as her son. I had every chance for education that her own daughters had. And I was so much younger than the girls that I'm sure she spoiled me."

When Guilford finished speaking, tears stung my eyes and I felt a kinship with the grandmother I had never known. At least I wasn't the only person who kept deathbed promises.

"I'm glad you told me about yourself," I said softly.

Guilford carried our empty glasses to the sideboard, then banked the embers of the fire and adjusted the flue. He turned out the lights behind us as we headed for our rooms.

On the stairway Guilford linked his arm through mine, and I made no protest. The warmth of his touch matched the warmth of my feeling for him. I felt drowsy and content.

At my doorway I looked into Guilford's eyes. "Thank you for talking to me. I appreciate your concern."

"You're quite welcome." Guilford squeezed my hand, then turned and left me.

Once inside my rooms I locked the door. A pleasant drowsiness drugged me, and before I fell asleep I understood Mrs. Foster's feeling for Guilford. His kindness and empathy made me forget his plain features. He had made a deep impression on me, and I looked forward to knowing him better.

CHAPTER SEVEN

Of course I overslept the next morning. When I awakened, a high fog masked the sun and sky and threw a gray pall over my suite. As I went down for breakfast I kept telling myself that last night's experience in Angela's suite had been a mistake, an accident. But only part of my mind believed.

Nobody was in the dining room, so I poked my head into the kitchen, where Tillie was washing dishes.

"Good morning, Tillie. Sorry I'm so late. Where is everyone?"

Tillie wiped her hands on her apron and poured me a glass of orange juice. "Miss Katherine is overseeing party preparations. Keeps the whole Lanrith family on the move, she does. Sir Henry was feeling a bit under, so he went back to his room. Mr. Dan's working. Mr. Guilford's gone to his London office. And Kimi and Mrs. Foster are arguing over Kimi's party dress."

"You really keep track of everyone," I said with a laugh.

Tillie plunked a bowl of porridge in front of me as I sat down at a worn worktable. I worried about Sir Henry. Did doctors come to so remote a spot? But of course they must.

Tillie chatted agreeably while I ate my porridge, but when I left the kitchen I felt at loose ends.

I went upstairs, and as I neared Kimi's door I heard the argument Tillie had mentioned. Kimi was in tears when I knocked.

"It can't be all that bad, Kimi," I said as Vinegar Face let me into the room. "Suppose you tell me your troubles."

Kimi broke into shuddering sobs and clung to my skirt.

"I'll tell you," Mrs. Foster said. "The brat wants a party dress just like her mother's, and Katherine refuses. Says she'll appear in no cow-and-calf costume. I've made the child a blue cotton, but she kicks and screams when I try it on her."

I almost choked on my anger. How dare Vinegar Face speak so harshly in front of Kimi! A glance at the dress in question told me that it was pretty enough. And I had an idea.

"Kimi!" I pulled her away from my skirt and tilted her chin so that she looked at me. "Your mother has a very special gown from Paris. It would be impossible to make you one just like it, but I'd like to wear a dress like yours."

"Really, Margo? Really?" Kimi smiled through her tears.

"Mrs. Foster, could you make me a similar dress?"

Mrs. Foster sighed. "I have to hand it to you. You know how to handle the child. There's material. I have time."

"Thank you. I'm no seamstress, but I could help on the cutting and the hemming and such." I turned to Kimi. "We'll be look-alike cousins. Won't that be fun!"

Kimi dried her tears, tried on her new dress, then ran outdoors to feed the toads.

Going to my room, I got paper and pen and decided to write. Merton Manor was an ideal spot for a writer — plenty of uninterrupted silence. I'll set up a personal writing schedule, I thought. I'll get my novel on its way. No one need know.

But this morning my mind refused to stay on my story characters. After a brief struggle I decided to take a walk. Slipping into a sweater, I left the manor by a back door, and Muldoon joined me as I idly headed toward the stables.

"Come along, boy," I invited. "Time for some exercise." At the stables the door Sir Henry and I had entered the day before was closed and bolted, so I went around to the other side of the building. Here another door was open, but a short distance away a small cemetery caught my eye. Muldoon headed toward it.

"Come back, Muldoon."

The dog ignored me. At first I hesitated, but then curiosity triumphed. I wandered over to examine the tombstones.

"They're like people," I said to Muldoon. "Some are tall and ornate, and others are small and plain."

The Merton name was everywhere. Sir William Merton. Mary Annette Wyclif Merton. Charles Henry Merton. I hardly noticed when Muldoon disappeared, I was so engrossed in the names.

Gooseflesh rose on my arms as I read my grandfather's name on one of the markers. His date of birth was engraved, and a space had been left for the date of his death.

I shuddered and pulled my sweater tighter about my shoulders. Was Angela buried here? I glanced around until I saw a new-looking grave marker, tall and wide and cut from umber marble.

As I walked toward the grave I jumped in surprise as Muldoon rose from behind it. I knew then that I had not been mistaken, and the inscription on the stone removed all doubt. Angela Elaine Merton Taledon had died five years ago at age twenty-five.

"Good morning."

Dan Taledon's voice startled me, and I whirled to face him, feeling like an intruder. Just for an instant a glint in Dan's eyes made me think that he had intended to frighten me, but the moment flicked by so quickly that I wondered if I had been mistaken. He carried a bouquet of pinks in a cream-colored pitcher that he placed on his wife's grave.

"Those are lovely." The empty comment rang false to my ears, but I didn't know what else to say. When Dan remained silent, I felt I had to shove more words into the void.

"I was just out for a stroll, and you did startle me. Tillie told me you were working."

"That I was." Dan glanced over his shoulder, but I was used to this mannerism by now. I ignored it.

"I decided to take a break," Dan said. "Sitting at a desk all morning becomes tedious. Sometimes a ride across the moor relaxes me."

"I should think this desolate spot would get to you." I relaxed a bit. "What do you do for entertainment?"

"I get into London or Cambridge once in a while, but for the most part I like to be alone. Would you care to go for a ride with me?"

"Then you got the Austin out of the mire?"

"Yes, it's out. The Lanriths did much of the work. But for right now I meant a horseback ride. Do you care for horses?"

"I'm not much of a rider, but I love horses. If you'll have me, I'll come along." I hoped I hadn't sounded too eager, but this brooding, silent man attracted me more than I cared to admit. Perhaps his very aloofness was a kind of challenge.

"Come on." Dan walked away from the cemetery, and Muldoon settled back down near Angela's grave.

The stallion snorted and reared as we entered the straw-scented stable, but the mare continued munching her grain.

"Quiet, Diablo. Easy does it." Dan patted the stallion's head. Then he lighted a lantern to dispel the gloom.

I knew by the way Dan handled the animals that he was an expert horseman. In no time he had both animals saddled and bridled and was leading them out onto the moor.

With ears flattened Diablo rolled his eyes and stamped the earth. Dan kept a tight grip on the reins.

"If you'll hold Genia and wait here a few moments, I'll give Diablo a short run just to fan the sparks from his system."

I nodded and watched as Dan mounted the stallion. Diablo streaked across the moorland as if he might never stop. After a few minutes Dan circled Diablo. He began with a large loop, then gradually squeezed the circles tighter and tighter. When he rejoined me, the stallion was considerably more calm.

"Can you mount?" Dan asked.

"I could if I had something to stand on." I looked around helplessly. "I'm used to a Western saddle. This English model offers no handhold."

Dan dismounted and gave me a leg up.

"Don't worry, Margo. We'll walk until you feel secure."

We headed away from the manor, following a trail that lay well back from the cliff's edge. Before long the manor was a mere speck on the horizon. I had no idea how far we had come.

The breeze had dispersed the fog, and from a group of low-hanging clouds a dramatic shaft of light fell on a tumble of rocks ahead of us.

"What's that?" I asked. "Surely nature didn't leave those rocks in such a position."

Dan smiled. "Thousands of years ago people came to this coast in boats with large leather sails. Today historians refer to them as tomb builders. Those rocks are one of their sites."

I shuddered. Was the whole day to be filled with graves and tombstones? "Where did these people come from?"

"Sir Henry has written a great deal about them," Dan replied. "He would be happy to give you all the details. According to his findings as a historian, it is believed that they came from the Mediterranean area, perhaps from Crete. They built quoits, or stone graves, from Cornwall to the north-west of Scotland. In a way they were like the ancient Egyptians. They lived in order to die."

The rocks were about fifty yards from the edge of the cliff, and I had no desire to explore them. I reined Genia toward the sea, where Atlantic rollers flung a lacework of foam onto the shore. I hadn't meant to ride so near to the edge, but Dan kept urging Diablo forward, and Genia stayed by his side.

In moments we stood at the brink of the precipice with the horses snorting and stamping their protest. Below us the sea bit and clawed at the granite cliffs. A few steps forward and we would plunge to our doom. Trembling, I reined Genia back, and as I did so, Dan pulled Diablo so close to me that our legs were touching. He leaned in his saddle, took Genia's reins from my hands, then kissed me.

CHAPTER EIGHT

I felt the pulse at my temple pounding, and I saw Dan through an angry red haze. Grabbing Genia's reins from his hands, I backed the mare from the precipice, turned her, and urged her toward the stable. Dan attracted me, but his actions were premature. He couldn't possibly be genuinely interested in me. Surely he had kissed me only because I reminded him of Angela. In that moment I hated my resemblance to my dead aunt.

Somehow I managed to cling to Genia's back as we cantered to the stable. Dan was at my side as I reined Genia to a stop, and I was glad that both horses were steaming. Dan had to rub them down; I was free to escape to the manor. Before I could protest, Dan helped me from the saddle, and while his strong hands were still around my waist, I saw Katherine watching us from an upper window.

As I walked toward the manor I pretended that I hadn't seen Katherine. I didn't look up. Inside, the whole house reeked of fish chowder, and when Sir Henry joined us at the table, I was glad to see that he was looking well.

"Did you have a good ride?" Katherine purred the words, but her blue eyes blazed.

"It was fine," I replied. "This countryside has a stark beauty even in its desolation."

"And you, Dan?" Katherine turned to her brother-in-law.

"As always," Dan replied.

"Now that you've been so refreshed, maybe you'll be able to get back to work this afternoon. My editor's demanding to see the beginning chapters of my next book." Katherine's voice was haughty and demanding, and I felt that I was the cause of her ire. Did she think that I had led Dan astray?

"Perhaps I could help you," I said. "I can type. With two of us working on the script, the copying would go much faster."

"That's unnecessary," Katherine responded with finality.

Why, I wondered, did she resent my being here? Did she think that I had come in quest of an inheritance?

Sir Henry began one of his long-winded tales, and I was relieved to have Katherine's attention distracted from me.

"This fish smell in here reminds me of the story about St. Ives," Sir Henry said. "Have I told you that one?"

Everyone began to squirm except Kimi, who always brightened when her grandfather told legends. Vinegar Face made an excuse to go to the kitchen, and I wondered if it was because Sir Henry's talk bored her or because Guilford wasn't here.

"St. Ives," Sir Henry said. "Margo, did you know that St. Ives is a real town?"

"I know now, but for years I thought St. Ives was just a place name in a nursery rhyme."

"St. Ives has a pollution problem." Sir Henry guffawed and pounded his cane on the carpet. "The place has a tendency to smell of fish. Oh, not always. But just sometimes when the winds and the tides are in a certain stage. And this is no legend. A Reverend Francis Kilvert was a diarist in the 1870's. He recorded that the Vicar of St. Ives confessed to him that the stench of fish in St. Ives was sometimes so strong that it stopped the church clock."

Sir Henry laughed and slapped his knee, and I found myself laughing with him. How I wished I could talk to him privately now, now when he was in a good mood and when his mind was clear.

As quickly as Sir Henry brought up the subject he dropped it and began talking about noises on the moor.

"I've never been frightened living among the bogs," he said, "but many fine people have."

"We've had quite enough legends for now," Katherine said. Sir Henry pouted, but Kimi broke the silence.

"Will you take me to the beach this afternoon, Margo?" she asked. "It's warm enough to wade, and the sun's out."

"Is it all right?" I looked at Katherine. "Is Kimi allowed to wade? I'd love to take her if it's okay."

"It's her nap time." Vinegar Face appeared, sounding her voice of doom. Kimi's face fell.

"Let the child wade." Sir Henry banged the floor with his cane and glared at Vinegar Face. "She'll sleep when she's tired. We should take advantage of the sun when it appears."

Kimi beamed at her grandfather, then clutched my hand. "Come on, Margo. I'll show you the way down to the sand."

"There's a shortcut to the beach," Katherine said. "Kimi knows where it is. Guilford's strung a rope to hang on to from the clifftop down to the sand. It'll save you a quarter of an hour's climbing time."

"Kimi?" I questioned.

"She's used to it, no problem."

I went upstairs and slipped into shorts and a shirt. When I met Kimi outside, she was dancing with excitement. "Hurry, Margo, hurry." She led the way to the hand rope.

"This path is almost straight up and down, Kimi!" Below us the blue-green water lapped and curled upon the sand.

"Don't look down and you won't get dizzy."

Only by following Kimi, by using the footholds she had memorized, by grasping the rope Guilford had provided, did I reach the sand beach without falling. Our arrival on the sand startled gulls and sandpipers, and I shaded my eyes from the sun's glare and watched as the birds soared on the breeze, screaming their protests.

"Since we've just eaten, we'd better walk for a few minutes before we go into the water," I said.

Kimi grinned. "I like to walk. I collect shells and pretty stones. I have a secret hiding place where I keep them."

"Is it so secret that you can't show me?" I asked.

She took my hand and pulled me toward the water, where the wet sand was packed and firm. Pausing at a spot where brown boulders jutted into the sea, she pointed.

"Look in that deep niche in the rocks. That's my secret place. No one else ever comes here."

I peered into the niche and touched some of Kimi's treasured shells. "They're beautiful, Kimi." As I held the shell I tried to rub out other footprints in the sand, footprints that proved the spot not so secret after all. Every child should grow up thinking that he or she has a secret place that no one else has discovered. All the while Kimi played with her special shells, I nonchalantly tried to blot out the footprints that led right to the rock she was sitting upon.

"Can we wade now?" Kimi asked.

I nodded, and then we waded into the water and played in the surf. I tasted the salt spray and felt the water icy-smooth against my legs. Kimi screamed in delight. Our feet and legs tingled with cold, but never had I seen a child so entranced.

"I hope you stay with us forever," Kimi said suddenly.

"But you know I'm just here for a short visit. I'll have to leave soon." I fingered the locket around my neck, wondering when I would have the opportunity to give it to Sir Henry.

"Don't go." Kimi looked up at me with tears in her eyes. "Please don't go."

"Maybe you can come to America to visit me someday."

"You're just saying that." Kimi stared across the sea. "I want you to stay. No one else ever brings me to the beach except Uncle Gil. And mostly he's away or too busy."

"But you've been here before," I said. "You showed me your secret place. You must come here a lot."

"Don't tell. I'm not supposed to come alone. Don't tell."

I made no promises. The day grew colder when I thought of Kimi here on this wild beach alone. Someone should know. Guilford? I wondered what Katherine was thinking of not to keep closer watch on her daughter.

"I'll race you to the top." Kimi dashed for the rope, not realizing that it was an unfair race. Only one could use the trail at a time. She scrambled up the cliff, and I waited until she was at the top before I started.

"I won! I won!" Kimi shouted as she reached the top.

I was on the cliffside about halfway between the sea and the moor when the rope gave way. Someone screamed, then everything went black.

CHAPTER NINE

As I regained consciousness I realized that the screams were splitting from my own throat. Then waves of nausea pounded me into silence. Yet the screaming continued. Screaming? No. Howling. Muldoon hunched beside me.

"Muldoon," I murmured. "Muldoon."

My head throbbed, and I felt a fluid stickiness warm my fingers when I reached to touch the worst area of pain. My left wrist was swollen and throbbing. With great effort I wiggled my toes. They worked. And so did my fingers. I remembered reading somewhere that if you could wiggle your toes and fingers your back wasn't broken. But maybe that was a fallacy. My back felt as if it were splintered in a dozen places.

When I finally managed to drag myself to a sitting position, Muldoon stopped howling and began licking my face.

"Muldoon! Go for help, Muldoon."

But Muldoon wouldn't budge. Bit by bit I remembered what had happened. The cliffside path. The rope. Kimi. Kimi!

I tried to stand, but my head swam and I

fell back onto the sand. Muldoon began howling again.

"Muldoon! Quiet!" My voice lacked authority, and the wolfhound paid no attention.

Great thick veils of fog were rolling in, and with the sun hidden, the air was chill and the beach formidable. Breakers battered the sand and rocks with relentless force. Each roaring wave brought the brine closer to me. Muldoon whined and tugged at my sleeve, demanding that I follow him.

"Can't do it, old boy." Muttering through clenched teeth, I managed to pull myself to a rock so I could lean back. Then I noticed a gash in my leg. Blood spurted from it.

I knew little of first aid, and my stomach churned at the sight of my own blood soaking into the sand. Somehow I managed to rip a cuff from my shorts, and common sense told me to tie it above the wound. I was intent on tying the makeshift tourniquet when I heard someone shouting my name.

Kimi! High above me the child stood at the edge of the cliff, pointing down. In a moment hands jerked her to safety.

"Margo!" Guilford called. "Hold on! I'm on my way down!"

In my mind I thanked Kimi for sounding

the alarm even though everyone from the manor now stood on the clifftop peering over at me. For once I was thankful for the fog. I hated to be seen in such frightful condition.

Peering upward, I could make out that Mrs. Foster now had Kimi in tow, and Tillie and Dan kept motioning Sir Henry to stand back farther. I saw Katherine's ebony cigarette holder and the glowing tip of her cigarette as she stalked back and forth like a cat on the prowl. I closed my eyes, embarrassed at being the center of so much attention.

It seemed hours before Guilford reached the beach.

"Don't try to move," he warned. "You may have broken bones."

"I've tested them," I said. "I think they all work. But I'm so weak I can hardly move."

"From loss of blood, from the looks of things," Guilford commented.

"How will I ever get back to the manor? And what are you doing here? I thought you were in London."

"Luckily I got sidetracked in Exeter."

I was so relieved just to have someone with me that I felt tears welling in my eyes.

With his body between me and the spectators on the clifftop, Guilford leaned over and kissed me gently on the lips.

"Can you stand?"

A moment ago I couldn't have, but now Guilford's eyes were magnets pulling me to my feet. Everything went black, and I thought I was going to vomit. Guilford steadied me against himself for a moment before he lifted me into his arms. I wrapped my uninjured right arm around his neck, rested my head on his shoulder, and welcomed the faint scent of turpentine that clung to his clothes. I was amazed at how such a common thing as a smell could give me a sense of security. Then I felt Guilford begin the ascent.

"I can't bear to look," I said.

"Then close your eyes."

I heard rocks thunder down the cliffside from where Guilford's shoes had loosened them. Once I felt him fall to his knees, but in a moment he was up again. Slowly and painstakingly he made his way to the clifftop.

I opened my eyes and smiled, but I could find no words to express my deep-felt thankfulness. Everyone crowded around.

"How did it happen?" Sir Henry demanded.

"Are you all right?" Tillie asked.

"Your arm's hurt," Kimi said, beginning to cry.

"You're frightening the child." Vinegar Face spoke as if I were deliberately trying to scare Kimi. She whisked her off into the fog, and I saw Tillie trying to restrain Sir Henry from moving closer to me.

"Margo! Margo! How did it happen?" He rested his weight on his cane as well as on Tillie's arm.

I tried to think, but my mind was fuzzy. How had it happened?

"The rope!" I said, remembering. "The rope broke. We were coming in. Kimi was already at the top."

Guilford and Dan made a chair of their arms and hands and carried me to the manor. I tried to keep my eyes open, focusing my gaze on the green pen behind Dan's ear. I heard Tillie and Sir Henry following us, and I saw Katherine hurrying on ahead.

The men took me to my room and left me in the care of Katherine and Vinegar Face.

"I'll have to cut this sleeve away in order to remove the blouse," Katherine said. "She has a nasty sprain."

"Good thing the bleeding's all stopped," Vinegar Face said, removing my tourniquet.

The two women talked to each other as if I were absent, and I sat lost in the aroma of lavender that hung in the room. Katherine snipped at the sleeve until it fell away, and when she removed the rest of the blouse from me, she caught the chain to my locket on her ring. The chain broke; the locket fell to the floor.

Mother's locket! Ignoring my pain, I leaned over to pick it up. Katherine grasped for it at the same moment, and our fingers touched, but Katherine's held the locket.

"Give it to me."

Katherine's face went livid as she stared at the bit of metal. Instead of putting it in my hand, she dropped it in the pocket of my blouse.

"Your hands are cut and scratched," Katherine said. "Mrs. Foster can't treat them while you're holding anything."

Vinegar Face applied iodine to my cuts and scrapes. My eyes watered from pain. This was the second time in as many days that I had been before these two women exposed and at disadvantage. I gritted my teeth against the stinging iodine.

"Let me help you into a fresh dress," Katherine said.

"Thank you, but I can manage," I replied.

Katherine nodded. "I'll take your things to the laundry." She picked up my blouse from the bed and started to leave.

"Wait." I forced myself to walk to her, to

retrieve the locket from my blouse. Katherine scowled and almost snatched the blouse from my hands. I felt sure that she had been trying to make off with the locket. But why? Why would she want it?

I felt better when the door closed behind the two women. My aunt Katherine's talent and ability drew me to her at the same time her egotism and cold manner repelled me. And her strange reaction to seeing my locket disturbed me. I didn't know how long I sat dozing in the chair before Tillie knocked.

"I've brought ye a cup of tea and a bowl of me best vegetable soup, miss. Try to eat a bit. It'll give ye strength."

I wasn't hungry, but I couldn't refuse Tillie after she had gone to all the trouble to make something special for me.

"I'll try the tea first." To my surprise I could almost feel strength trickling back into my battered body. The smell of the soup soon persuaded me to start eating.

"It's delicious, Tillie. Thank you so much."

"Ye be welcome, miss."

"Why do Mrs. Foster and Katherine dislike me so, Tillie?" I blurted the question as I spooned the soup. "They do, you know. I can tell. But I don't know why. What have I done?"

"Ye've done nothing, miss," Tillie replied. "Nothing."

"But I must have done something. Surely they don't find my resemblance to Angela so upsetting that they must be unfriendly."

When I looked up from the soup, Tillie was wiping her eyes.

"Tillie! What is it? Why are you crying?"

Tillie moved closer and whispered in my ear. "Take care, miss. I think that ye may be in grave danger."

"What sort of danger? I don't understand."

"There is talk that Miss Angela was murdered, Miss Margo. And I just feel it in me bones that ye might be in danger."

"Nobody's told me this about Angela before," I said, reluctant to listen to servants' gossip. "Mr. Guilford said that she had an accident, that she fell over the cliff."

"That is true." Tillie nodded vigorously. "And the authorities from Bodrevy Village came to investigate. They said Angela's death was an accident, but the talk goes on just the same, and I've never even breathed a word of what I know to be fact."

"What do you know?" I asked the question never really thinking that Tillie was going to reveal anything of import.

"Miss Margo, I do like ye. And I trust ye.

Few Mertons would come into me kitchen just like common folk and share recipes and cooking secrets. You're something special. I'll tell ye what I saw with me own eyes. But let it go no farther than these walls."

I nodded.

"The Bodrevy authorities think that no one saw Miss Angela fall over the cliff. But I saw. And so did Mr. Dan."

I liked Tillie. She didn't play it coy, pausing in the dramatic spots, making me ask her for every detail. She just told her story straight out, and I believed every word of it.

"Miss Angela was sitting out there at the edge of the cliff. Sitting on the logan stone and rocking like she always did in the early evenings. I saw Mr. Dan head out that way to fetch her inside. I don't know whether or not she heard him. She didn't look around. Then the next thing I knew, the logan stone rocked too far. I could hardly believe me eyes. It teetered sort of crazy like. Up, back then up, up, up — like a slow-motion film. And it went over the cliff."

There was a long silence in which neither of us spoke. Then I asked the question that screamed through my mind.

"Did Dan push her?"

"That's not for me to say, miss." Tillie

wrung her hands. "I know he was close enough to touch her, but I couldn't say that he did touch her. I couldn't see for sure from where I stood."

"But why have you kept this a secret?"

"There never was any trial. The authorities never asked what I saw. And Mr. Dan never said anything about being with her at the last. He ran to the manor and ducked inside the back door. He acted as surprised as anything when a fisherman came shouting the terrible news to us. It wasn't me place to speak up, ma'am. It wasn't me place to put Mr. Dan in a bad spot. I wouldn't have told ye this except for your own good."

Tillie's confiding mood ended. I had finished eating, and as she took my tray and left the room she seemed to take the room's warmth with her. I shivered and drew my robe more tightly about me. Had Tillie known that I had been riding with Dan this morning? Was she trying to warn me against him?

Reliving the moments when Dan and I sat on our horses perilously close to the edge of the cliff, I shuddered and hid my face behind my hands. Was Dan Taledon a murderer! But how unfair of me to suspect him of such a thing. I had no business listening to servants' talk. Yet Tillie had been so sincere that it was impossible to doubt her. She planted seeds of distrust in my mind. Dan Taledon, who had attracted me so, now frightened me.

Tillie's food had given me strength, and I was about to try to walk to my bed when another knock sounded on my door.

"Who's there?" I called.

"Guilford."

"Come in."

Guilford opened the door with one hand, and with the other he balanced an elaborate board with a replica of Merton Manor mounted upon it. Muldoon followed him.

"What on earth!" I exclaimed. I didn't want any more conversation that evening, yet I hated to hurt Guilford's feelings. I hadn't even been able to thank him properly for rescuing me.

Guilford rested his miniature on the sofa. "This was just a ruse to distract anyone who might have seen me come in here. I wanted to be sure you are all right. I telephoned the doctor in the village, but he's out on an emergency call."

"I'll be all right. A good night's sleep will work miracles."

"But that wrist." Guilford motioned for me to let him examine my arm. Although his fingers probed only lightly, pain shot to my shoulder.

"I think it's only a sprain." Guilford's face grew sober. "You're going to dislike what I have to say, but I believe that someone may have deliberately cut that rope that let you fall down the cliff."

"Guilford!"

"Now, wait. I'm not sure. I'm merely suspicious. I'll get the rope and have a look at it tomorrow. It's too foggy and dark to risk hunting for it tonight."

"I don't understand. Yesterday when I was scared to bits over being locked in Angela's rooms, you were the one who convinced me the whole affair had been an accident."

"Yesterday I believed that," Guilford said. "But two accidents in two days! I'll leave Muldoon with you as a guard tonight — then first thing tomorrow I'll do some checking. If you keep Muldoon at your side and your door locked, nothing can harm you."

"Last night's trick about the locked door might have been an accident, or it might have been a ploy intended just to frighten me. But this! Kimi and I could both have been killed."

The overhead light cast interesting

shadows on Guilford's craggy face. "You're right. That's why I came here to warn you. I may be wrong. This whole thing may have been another accident. But no one was ever hurt by being cautious."

CHAPTER TEN

Although Guilford had said that showing me his miniature of Merton Manor was a ruse, he was eager to display it. I asked him about it to take my mind off the horrible thing he had just suggested, and he needed little prompting.

"This manor's about to fall down around our ears." Guilford lifted the roof and the second story from his scale model. "There have been no major changes since Sir Henry's wife had the kitchen modernized years ago. Now, what do you think of this?"

"I don't understand it." With an effort I banished fatigue from my voice.

"I've redesigned the living-room alcove into a small suite for Sir Henry." Guilford pointed out that change. "He has no business climbing those stairs every day. By using screens for dividers I could section off one end of the drawing room to be used as a library for both Sir Henry and Katherine."

"That sounds like a good plan," I said. "And what are these rooms by the kitchen?"

"Storage pantries. But I think it would be more practical to turn them into rooms for

Mrs. Foster and Tillie and to convert the whole third floor into a grand ballroom. This would also hold Katherine's memorabilia."

"When are you going to make all these changes?"

"Probably never." Guilford replaced the top on the miniature with a faraway look in his eye. "Sir Henry has approved all of my plans, but Katherine refuses to give her okay. Her father will never go against her wishes; Katherine's used to having things her way, and she hates to spend money."

I disliked hearing about a family quarrel, and I was so tired that I was glad when Guilford picked up his model manor and prepared to leave my suite.

"I empathize with you, Guilford. Your ideas are good. Sir Henry is lucky to have a decorator-artist in the family."

"The manor's lovely, but it's showing signs of wear, and the space could be used to better advantage. But don't get me started again. Good night, Margo."

Guilford let himself out of the suite, and I locked the door behind him. After viewing the miniature I could see why Guilford was a success in his field. He had creative talent quite equal to Katherine's. Perhaps that was why they didn't get on so well; perhaps there was too much striving between them.

As I struggled into bed, Muldoon stirred. I patted his head. I had almost forgotten the real reason for Guilford's visit. The rope. I sighed and vowed not to become unduly upset. I would worry tomorrow if I found that such concern was necessary. In the meantime I considered plans to leave the manor, to cut my visit short. I had to leave as soon as possible. Dan Taledon attracted me more than I liked to admit, and my sympathies also went out to Guilford. But I felt a hostility here at Merton Manor that I couldn't pinpoint.

What had I got myself into? I had no intention of falling for my foster uncle or for a man under suspicion of murder. But what about Katherine's party? I wanted to meet England's literary people; I might learn something that would benefit my own writing career. Shortly after the celebration I would make excuses to return to New York. But before I left, I would return the locket to Sir Henry. I promised myself that.

Fog hung heavy over the moor when I awakened the following morning. No nightmare had disturbed my sleep and I was glad of that, but now I felt hemmed in, felt as if the world came to an end in the gray murk right outside my window. Muldoon rose from his place by the door as I began to stir.

I felt stiff and sore from my fall, but the swelling in my left wrist had gone down. My head still pulsed with a throbbing pain. Going downstairs was a challenge to my leg muscles.

"Good morning," I greeted Guilford outside the dining room. He wore jeans and a turtleneck sweater, and I wondered if he had been painting so early in the morning.

"I tried to find the rope, but it was gone," he whispered and shook his head. "I suspected foul play, but when I inquired around, I learned that Mr. Lanrith took it."

"But why? Surely Mr. Lanrith has nothing to hide. Can you find where he put it? You could still examine it."

"I was too late." Guilford touched my elbow and guided me into the drawing room, where we could talk aloud. "Mr. Lanrith said that he burned the rope. He acted innocent enough. He said that he knew we wouldn't want it lying around with the big party being tomorrow and all. And since it had given way once, he knew it was a menace as a handrail."

"But did he examine it?"

"I asked him that. I hated to reveal my suspicions, but there was no other way. He said he paid no particular attention, that it looked as if friction against a rock had cut it to pieces."

"Then I'll accept that explanation." I turned and headed for the dining room. "I hate to suspect people, but, Guilford, I do appreciate your concern."

I spoke with more calmness than I felt. Whom could I trust or confide in? Only the thought that I was leaving soon sustained me. Surely if everyone knew that I was going, nothing else out of the ordinary would happen to me.

My opportunity to make my announcement came when Charles Lanrith brought the mail to Sir Henry just before we sat down at the breakfast table.

"A letter for you, Margo." Katherine handed me a thin blue envelope and went on sorting the others.

"Thank you, Aunt Katherine." My letter was from Julia, and I read it hastily. I made the most of it a few minutes later when Sir Henry inquired if all was well in New York.

"I'm afraid I have rather bad news," I lied. "My cousin is ill. She'll have to be in the hospital for exploratory surgery. I'm sorry, but there's nothing for me to do but return home to be with her. She has no other family."

"But the party!" Kimi shrilled. "You have

to stay for the party. Please, oh, please!"

I thought of Kimi and of the dresses we planned to wear, and I pretended to scan my letter once more.

"If I leave London the afternoon following the party, I'll arrive home soon enough."

Kimi's smile was worth a hundred thank-yous.

"I'm sorry your visit will be cut short." Katherine pulled a creased napkin from beneath her place mat. "It really seems that you've only arrived."

I met my aunt's direct gaze. She looked sincere enough, but somehow her words rang false. Dan and Guilford said nothing. It was Sir Henry who, like Kimi, was truly upset.

"We've barely had time to get acquainted," he said. "We must surely spend this day together if you feel up to it."

I tried to pretend that my head had quit aching as I nodded in agreement. This would be my chance to return the locket. Today. Facing Katherine, I gathered all my courage. I had no intention of begging for favors, but I had to speak one more time.

"It would mean a great deal to me if you would grant me even a short interview, Aunt Katherine. I would gladly let you edit anything I wrote about you. In addition to giving me a boost in a most competitive field, a stateside article about you would give you a great deal of excellent publicity."

"Such an idea is preposterous. Entirely impossible!" Katherine spat the words, and I was sorry I had approached the subject again. But Sir Henry spoke up.

"I'll tell you anything you want to know about your aunt Katherine, Margo." He rapped his cane on the floor for emphasis. " 'A Father Speaks of His Famous Daughter.' How's that for a title?"

My hope sprang anew. This was a different approach.

"Would you object to that, Aunt Katherine?"

"Is there no stopping you!" Katherine's eyes blazed. "Who do you think will believe a man who talks to toads?"

Katherine flounced from the table without excusing herself, and I flushed. Why couldn't I accept no for an answer!

After breakfast Guilford motioned me aside once again.

"Take care, Margo. I don't want to frighten you, but you may be in danger."

"I'm spending the morning with Sir Henry," I replied. "I'm sure I'll be all right."

"Keep Muldoon at your side," Guilford

insisted. "I'll be working in my suite today. Call immediately if you need me."

Guilford's plain features were so clouded with concern that I promised.

"Come, Muldoon," I called. "Come with me."

Sir Henry greeted me at his door and invited me inside. He showed me his books, his diplomas, his honorary degrees, but he had only half of my attention. Part of my mind searched for a way to present him the locket. I trembled as I broached the subject.

"Sir Henry, my mother loved her family."

"If that's true, she would never have left us." Sir Henry gazed out the window.

For a moment I touched Muldoon's head for moral support. "Her last thoughts were of you. I know you've wondered why I came here. I came at her request."

"When it was too late," Sir Henry murmured. "Far too late."

"Perhaps it's never too late for love and forgiveness." I took the locket from my skirt pocket and held it toward Sir Henry. I dropped it into his hand. "My mother's last wish was that I bring this locket to you. I have never opened it, but it seemed to contain something very important to her."

Sir Henry turned the locket over and over in his gnarled hands; then at last he opened it and held it toward me.

"The picture is of myself and your grand-mother, and the sand in the other side came from the beach here at the manor."

I tried to hide my disappointment.

"I gave each of my daughters identical gold lockets on their sixteenth birthdays. When Wanda left Merton Manor, she took only the clothes she wore and her locket. She showed it to me that last day and asked my forgiveness for leaving. I can remember the exact scene after all these years. The whole family was gathered for tea in the alcove. Wanda looked directly at me and said, 'I am in love and I must go. I take nothing except your picture and some Cornish sand to remind me of home.' "

"And you let her go just like that?" I asked.

Sir Henry nodded. "I was proud and haughty and hurt. I told her that the day would come when she would regret her actions. I told her that when a Merton dropped that locket back into my hand, I would forgive her."

"A Merton has dropped it into your hand. I'm glad you've told me all this. I understand both you and my mother better."

I liked this proud old man, and I knew that my mother must have loved him. How it must have broken her heart to have ended all association with England and her family. Now that the locket was in Sir Henry's possession, I felt a sense of relief and freedom, freedom to return to New York. My steps were light as I accompanied Sir Henry to lunch.

At the table Kimi begged to go wading. "Take me, Katherine. Please. The fog's gone. There's sunshine."

"Absolutely not," Katherine replied. "There's too much to be done to prepare for the party."

I was certainly in no condition to take the child to the beach, and my heart ached for her. What a lonely life she led on this moor with no playmates to share her fun and her secrets.

After lunch I decided to take a nap. My throbbing head and my aching bones and muscles begged for a rest. It was almost tea-time when I awakened, feeling rested and refreshed. I decided that this would be a good time to apologize to Katherine for trying to invade her privacy, so with Muldoon at my heels I walked down the corridor to her rooms. I had raised my hand and was about to knock on her door when I heard her typewriter. Respecting her need for privacy, I returned to my own room.

From my window I gazed at the beach, and I smiled as I saw Katherine tramping through the sand.

"She's taken time to play with Kimi after all," I said, patting Muldoon's head. I stood on tiptoe trying to catch a glimpse of Kimi, but she was nowhere in sight. Instead I saw Dan scowling into Katherine's laughing face. When I heard Kimi running down the stairs, I was puzzled.

It was none of my business, but I wondered who was in Katherine's room typing. Guilford? But that was none of my concern. For the next hour I busied myself packing for my trip home. When I could pack no more, I called to Muldoon.

"Come, fellow, let's see if it's teatime." As I walked by Dan's room I stopped to pick up a Pepto wrapper. To my surprise Dan opened his door.

"Teatime?" he asked. I nodded.

Muldoon padded downstairs with us. Tillie had prepared a lovely tea, but Dan and I were the only ones who settled ourselves by the fireplace to enjoy it.

"Sir Henry and Kimi are taking tea in Sir Henry's suite," Tillie said. "Katherine's gone for a walk, and Guilford drove to the village on business."

"So we'll have tea for two." Dan smiled at

me. "I rather like that idea. Bring our tray into the alcove, Tillie. I'll light the fire on that hearth."

Dan attracted me, yet at the same time he frightened me. Why? I tried not to let Tillie's tale influence my thinking, but I reached down to pat Muldoon, glad that he was staying near me.

The fire crackled and popped, and the pungent odor of wood smoke made me cough.

"Sorry, Margo," Dan said. "I'll adjust the chimney vent."

By the time Tillie left us alone my hands were shaking so badly that my teacup rattled against its saucer. I tried to steady myself, but the likeness of Angela staring down at me from her gold-framed portrait did nothing to calm me.

"Perhaps we should have remained by another fireside," Dan said, as if he could read my mind. "You must find your resemblance to Angela disconcerting; I have no doubt that you've heard the murder rumors by now."

Had Dan brought me here to frighten me? "I've heard them, but I put no stock in such talk. Who would have wanted to murder my aunt? From what I've heard, everyone loved her."

"The husband is always the first suspect." Dan's eyes bored into me.

"I pronounce the husband innocent." I kept my voice light and somehow managed to sip my tea without rattling the cup and saucer. "Who is next on the suspect list?"

"How about Guilford?" Dan's tone took on the same bantering quality as mine. But murder was no joking matter; the brooding look in his eyes belied his facetiousness.

"Why Guilford?" I asked. "What motive would he have had?"

Dan shrugged. "He stands to share the Merton fortune on Sir Henry's death. At least, that's how things stood before you arrived. Sir Henry's old and he's ill. He can't live much longer. Maybe Guilford's afraid that you'll receive your mother's share of the estate."

Again I shivered as I thought of the waiting grave in the family burial plot and the frail old man with the wandering mind. "I didn't come here for money."

"Sir Henry has taken a liking to you," Dan said. "It's quite obvious. And I certainly can't blame him. You're lovely, you know. And who can guess what Sir Henry might do? A will can always be changed — as long as the person is living, that is."

"Are you insinuating that my staying here

might endanger Sir Henry's life?" I asked.

"Your staying or leaving would matter little. A will can be changed no matter where you are. But if you were dead . . ."

"You think I'm in danger?" I met Dan's steady gaze, refusing to let him know he was frightening me.

"Guilford needs money to go into the interior decorating business for himself. I have no proof that Guilford is guilty, but Angela's death brought him a bit closer to his goal. And now your Mother's death . . . Well, figure it out for yourself."

"I know that Guilford wants to own his own business. He says so quite openly." Hadn't Guilford already pointed out to me that I was a financial threat to Katherine? But what Dan said carried seeds of truth. Guilford might feel financially threatened by my sudden appearance in Cornwall. I scowled. It was terrible to know that people had reason to hate me.

"Margo! Margo!" Kimi rushed into the room. "The dresses are finished. Come try yours on and let's see how we look together." Kimi wore her party dress, and the delicate blue was a perfect foil for her dark hair and fair coloring. I silently thanked Kimi for breaking up my conversation with Dan.

"Excuse me, Dan. I really must try on the dress. Mrs. Foster has worked so hard on it."

"Of course." Dan rose, and as I followed Kimi I could feel his eyes boring into my back. In those few moments I almost hated him. How dare he insinuate that Guilford had murdered Angela! I didn't want to face that possibility any more than I wanted to face the possibility that Dan was pointing a finger at Guilford in an effort to keep himself in the clear.

Was there no one in this house I could trust! Obviously Dan had been trying to warn me that I was in danger. He hadn't come straight out and said it as Tillie had. Perhaps he was just jealous of Guilford and was trying to discredit him in my eyes. But surely that was a delusion of grandeur on my part. I seldom galvanized men to jealousy.

"I said do you like my dress?" Kimi demanded my attention.

"It's lovely, and it makes you look so grown up." I smiled at Kimi, but so many ideas whirled in my head that I felt dizzy.

I had announced my plans to leave Merton Manor following the party, and I had no real reason to change my mind and go sooner. I vowed to order my own life. I would not be defeated by ungrounded fears. Kimi would have her big moment, appearing at the party dressed just like a grown-up. But I could hardly wait to leave the Mertons and Cornwall.

CHAPTER ELEVEN

After dinner Sir Henry and I went to his suite, where we visited late into the night as if trying to make up for a lifetime of separation in a few short hours. I would have slept late the next morning, but Kimi awakened me shortly after sunrise.

"They're here, Margo! They're here!" she shouted outside my door.

I got up; I let Kimi in. The sound of voices and laughter drifted to my window from the lawn, and we rushed to pull the draperies and peer outside.

"Are the guests arriving at this hour?" I asked. "I thought it was to be an afternoon buffet."

"Mrs. Foster hires people from the village to help her," Kimi said. "They're more fun than the real company."

People streamed toward the house. Women clutched their black shawls about their shoulders, and three girls in cotton housedresses undulated across the terrace, fully aware of the male eyes upon them. As one young buck snapped a red bandanna, stinging a plump blonde on her backside, the older men laughed and spit streams of tobacco juice into the cracks between the flagstones.

"Enough noise! Give me your attention." Vinegar Face broke into the general merriment.

"She'll make them change clothes," Kimi said. "Then they'll all look the same. I like them better this way."

We waited until the last of the hired help was inside, and then Kimi sat on the edge of the bed while I dressed and combed my hair. Together we hurried downstairs for breakfast. I had expected a great clamor in the drawing room, but all was quiet.

"They've gone to the storage rooms to change clothes," Kimi said. Then, glancing into the dining room, she exclaimed, "Oh, Margo! Look at the flowers."

"Gladioli. Peonies. Roses." Everywhere I looked there were huge bouquets. Their scent perfumed the air, and I was like a child in my desire to touch the velvet-soft petals. The room radiated color and fragrance. I felt myself forgetting my fears and slipping into a party mood.

"No proper breakfast this morning, Miss Margo," Tillie announced when we entered the kitchen. She wiped her flour-smudged hands on her ample apron front, and her cheeks gleamed like polished apples. "Help yourself to dry cereal from that tray by the sink."

I helped Kimi pour cream over her wheat flakes, but when I finished, she was too excited to eat. I made them my own breakfast.

A crash in the dining room brought us both to our feet. We hurried through the doorway to see Tillie and three extra table leaves in a heap on the floor.

"Tillie! Are you hurt?" I shoved the polished wooden slabs aside and helped Tillie to her feet just as Vinegar Face appeared on the scene with her many helpers all uniformed and in a single file behind her.

"No harm done, ma'am," Tillie assured Mrs. Foster. She retrieved her slipper, which had skittered across the floor. Her face flushed brick-red, and I longed to ease her feelings.

"Humph!" Mrs. Foster snorted. "How can I trust you with a punch bowl when you can't even carry table leaves properly?"

"Indeed it won't happen again, ma'am."

"She needn't be so nasty," I said to Kimi. "But she is efficient. I don't see how she managed to transform that unpromising crew of villagers into a uniformed staff of servants." The workers had already received their orders, for they flew to their tasks with few questions asked.

"Men!" Vinegar Face clapped her hands. "Clear the dining room of excess furniture and be quick about it. The guests must have plenty of room to pass before the buffet table."

"Yes, ma'am." The men nodded and went to work. A few moments later Vinegar Face raised her voice again.

"Charles! Don't move that chair away from the window."

Charles Lanrith set the heavy leather-upholstered chair back down as if it were light as a daisy petal.

"No. Don't leave it there, either." Vinegar Face shoved at the chair. "This's Mr. Guilford's special chair, and he likes it right here by the window where he can have a view of the sea."

"I'll take charge of the table centerpiece," Katherine said, entering the room. One by one she stacked a collection of her books in a clever arrangement that formed her initials. I had never noticed it before, but the dust jackets were all printed in variations of her favorite colors: blue, black, and tan.

The hours passed like minutes. When Tillie began bringing the special morsels she had been working on for days from the kitchen to the buffet table, I knew it was past time for Kimi and me to get dressed.

"We'd better hurry. Let's dress in my suite." By prearrangement with Vinegar Face I was allowed to help Kimi dress. She took a quick bath while I did my hair. When she appeared fresh from the tub, I helped her into her dress.

"Now, but don't you look grand!" I pushed Kimi in front of a full-length mirror on my closet door.

"My dress is beautiful. Hurry and put yours on."

"You're the one who's beautiful." I guided her to the couch. "You sit here while I get ready."

I took but a moment slipping into my dress, and Kimi and I were both pleased with the results of Vinegar Face's sewing. But there was little time left to chat. We hurried downstairs to take our places in the reception line as Katherine had planned.

Of course Katherine, resplendent in her Paris creation, stood in the place of honor. Then came Kimi and Sir Henry. Guilford was next, and I stood on his right. Next to me Dan waited in brooding silence.

"Didn't know we were to have live music." I nodded toward a bass player, a pianist, and a drummer who had set up a bandstand near the alcove.

"Katherine thinks of everything," Dan said. "Everything."

Greeting the guests wasn't as bad as I had feared it might be. They seemed like a friendly lot, although I couldn't sort the editors from the critics or the publishers. As it turned out, Kimi drew the lion's share of attention from the arriving dignitaries. When the reception line broke up, Katherine accosted Vinegar Face.

"The child goes to bed just as soon as she has eaten," Katherine said. "This is an adult party, not a baby show."

"I'll see to it, ma'am." Vinegar Face took Kimi in tow.

I enjoyed meeting the elite of the British publishing world, and the buffet ended long before I realized how much time had passed. Now what? No one had mentioned what Katherine had planned for the entertainment of her guests other than dancing, but I wasn't kept in suspense for long.

Two servants appeared carrying a tape recorder. They set it up while Katherine made an announcement.

"In complying with your many requests, I have made a recording of excerpts from my forthcoming book, *Trumpets and Drums*. If everyone will make himself comfortable, we will listen together."

Kimi, seeing her mother apart from the crowd, ran to her and clutched her skirt. "Katherine! Katherine! Don't let Mrs. Foster take me away. Not yet."

Mercifully the musicians began to play. Katherine loosened Kimi's grip from her skirt and smoothed the material. Then jerking Kimi by the wrist, she dragged her to Vinegar Face, who was standing near me.

"I told you to put her to bed." Katherine's eyes blazed.

Kimi began kicking and screaming, utterly exhausted from the excitement of the day.

"Let me take her," I said. "Kimi, will you come with me?"

Kimi's tears subsided. "Hold my hand, Margo."

I took her hand, and we were just turning to leave the drawing room when the musicians stopped playing and Katherine's recording started. All voices hushed. The amplifiers hummed. Then the sound of a typewriter filled the room.

Katherine muttered at the men in charge of the recorder, "You idiots! Can't you do anything right?" She rushed forward and snapped the recorder off, jerked away the offending tape, and replaced it with another. After a brief pause her reading voice purred into the room to an attentive audience.

Suddenly something puzzled me. Had Katherine taped the sound of typing to make someone think she was working in her suite when in reality she was elsewhere? But who would she be trying to fool? And why? I mulled over the first thought that darted to my mind.

Was Katherine using the recording to cover for her while she was secretly meeting someone? Katherine was the dramatic type who would thrive on intrigue and clandestine meetings.

"Do I have to take off my dress?" Kimi demanded my attention.

"You wouldn't want to muss it sleeping in it, would you?"

Kimi shook her head, and once we reached my rooms, she undressed and fell asleep almost before I could get her into the bed. I tiptoed down the back stairway to the kitchen.

"Here, Muldoon," I called. The wolfhound seemed glad enough to come with me to my room, and I knew Kimi would welcome seeing him when she awakened in the strange suite.

The party ground on and on. The recording ended. People began dancing.

Other guests departed. More guests arrived. Tillie kept the buffet table replenished, and Vinegar Face managed the behind-the-scenes help. I had just stepped outside for a moment's respite when Guilford called to me.

"May I join you?"

"But I'm not going anywhere." Tonight the scent of a lemony after-shave lotion replaced the paint-and-turpentine odor that frequently traveled with Guilford.

"This affair's always a crashing bore," Guilford said. "Let's go for a walk. We won't be missed. Katherine's holding forth at one end of the drawing room, and Sir Henry has a captive audience at the other end."

Taking my elbow, Guilford guided me down the well-worn path toward the stable, and when we had put the building between us and the manor, he dropped down into the soft grass and pulled me down beside him. We sat there for a long time without speaking, just gazing at the sea and sky and feeling the stout timbers of the stable against our backs. Here in this peaceful spot I could believe none of the insinuations Dan had made against Guilford. I was sure that he was as open and aboveboard as he seemed. Or at least I was almost sure. I wished I could extinguish the doubt that lingered.

"You must have guessed how I feel," Guilford said, breaking the silence. "I'm in love with you, Margo. Totally and completely in love."

Guilford pulled me toward him and kissed me with a strength and tenderness I had never known before. It was all I could do to force myself to pull away from him.

"Stop, Guilford. Please stop."

"You love me, don't you?" Guilford squeezed my hand until it hurt. "Can you deny that you love me?"

I knew I couldn't deny my love for Guilford, but neither could I admit it just yet. What if he was a murderer? I searched my heart for an answer. But I had time to neither deny nor affirm my feelings, for at that moment Tillie called my name.

"Miss Margo! Miss Margo!"

Guilford stood and pulled me to my feet.

"Miss Margo!" Tillie called again.

"What is it, Tillie?" I asked as Guilford and I made an appearance from behind the stable.

After I spoke I noticed that Tillie's face was a mask of fright and sorrow. "It's Sir Henry!" she cried. "He's had some sort of attack. Mrs. Foster has summoned a doctor and the guests are leaving, but Sir Henry is calling for you."

"For me?"

"Well, I'm sorry, Miss Margo, but he's calling for Angela. I thought that perhaps, perhaps ye would . . ."

I knew what Tillie wanted me to do, and I went with her. If my presence would help Sir Henry, it didn't matter who he thought I was. For once I was glad that I looked like Angela.

CHAPTER TWELVE

Three weeks later, long after my intended departure date, I was still at Merton Manor. I had pretended to the family that Julia's surgery had been postponed, for my duty was here with my grandfather. Sir Henry's needs regulated my hours and my days.

The decision to stay and be of service had been mine; nobody forced me to remain. I was no longer a scrap of paper being tossed by the wind.

"Miss Margo." Tray in hand, Tillie paused at the doorway to my suite. "Sir Henry's lunch is ready."

"Good. I'll take it to him." Closing my door behind me, I followed Tillie to Sir Henry's quarters. The room smelled like a medicine chest, and I opened a window to air it out.

"Angela!" Sir Henry's voice wavered. "I knew you'd come soon. Where have you been?"

"In my room," I replied. "Are you hungry?"

Sir Henry sighed and turned his head away, but I paid no attention.

"The doctor says you're much better today," I said. "Day by day you're over-coming the effects of your stroke."

"High time," Sir Henry muttered, vigor returning to his voice. "Do I smell stew again?"

"It's lamb stew." I tried to sound enthusi-astic even though the meat smelled a lot like a damp sweater. "And there's gelatin. Strawberry. Your favorite flavor. It'll give you strength."

Sir Henry allowed me to feed him a few bites, and then for the first time since his stroke, he tried to feed himself.

"You're doing fine! I'm proud of you."

Sir Henry sighed. "I'm tired. Angela, you feed me, will you?"

I took the spoon and fed him the rest of his meal. Being called Angela was beginning to have a strange effect on me. More and more often I tried to imagine what my aunt had been like. And of course I wondered if someone really had hated her enough to murder her.

I could never quite shake off the nagging fear that I might be endangering my own life by feeding my grandfather. I felt he would die from starvation if he thought his pre-cious Angela had deserted him. Tillie's words about Dan still lurked in my mind.

And Dan's words about wills and legacies haunted me. Perhaps someone really did want Sir Henry dead. But surely I was safe as long as my grandfather's mind was clouded. He couldn't change his will in his present state.

"Angela, have I told you the legend of Langarrow?"

"No, I don't believe that you have."

"Do you have time to listen? I'm planning to include it in my book."

"Of course I'll listen." It puzzled me that a person could live in the past and the future at the same time. Angela had died years ago, yet the legend book was a thing of to-morrow. Time was a muddle in Sir Henry's head, and I wondered if he would ever again live in the present. After he finished telling his legend, I spoke.

"It's an interesting tale. Would you like me to bring you paper and pen so you can write it down?"

My grandfather shook his head. "Not now. My strength went in the telling. To-morrow I'll put it on paper."

Tomorrow. Always tomorrow.

Everyone was finished eating by the time I reached the dining room, but Tillie had laid a tray for me. After thanking her I carried it out to a lawn chair on the terrace in front of the manor. Clouds were rising like gray yeast dough, but enough sunlight filtered through them to warm me.

"May I join you?" Dan pulled a chair up beside mine. "I think you must be avoiding me, I so seldom see you."

"Sir Henry keeps me very busy," I hedged, trying not to flush at the truth in Dan's words. Ever since his insinuations against Guilford, I had tried to keep Dan at a distance.

"You shouldn't let the old man tie you down so. You came here for a vacation."

"But my plans changed," I reminded him. "Sir Henry needs me. He has only his memories of Angela."

As I set my lunch tray aside, Dan reached over and clasped my hand. "Listen to me, Margo. Don't you know that I care a great deal for you? I had no right to force myself on you weeks ago while we were riding. I apologize for that. But I've bided my time long enough. I must speak."

My mind raced, searching for a way to divert Dan's thoughts. He was handsome. And he fascinated me. But I wanted no declarations of his love. He frightened me. I was willing to pinch-hit for Angela for her father, but never for her husband.

"I care for you, Dan, just as I care for the

others I've become involved with here at the manor. You are my only family. But I have commitments in New York. Please try to understand."

"I get the message." Dan sighed, and I saw his hands clench into fists. I was nonplussed. I certainly didn't want to hurt him, but neither did I want to lead him on. But why? Four weeks ago I could have fallen madly in love with Dan. I tried to analyze my feelings.

Ralph had left a wide gap in my life, and I had almost fallen for Dan at first sight. His smoldering eyes, his brooding face, and his intriguing silence had been a challenge to me. I had felt a desire to be needed by such a man as he.

But all that was past. Had Tillie's words come between us? For days I had tried to tell myself that this was the case, but I had been lying to myself. Guilford was the one who had come between us. I knew in this moment that in spite of my best intentions I was deeply in love with Guilford although he had said little more to me since the day of Katherine's party.

"Please excuse me, Dan," I said. "It's grown chilly; I need a sweater."

"Of course." Dan sighed. I saw a desperate look in his eyes, and I felt threatened.

I hurried to my room and closed the door and stood staring out at the sea.

I don't know if it was the pulsing surf or the reflection of splintered sunlight against water, but I was drawn to the beach. The crazy thought wheeled through my mind that from the other side of the vale, Angela was willing me to her death site.

"Muldoon, Muldoon!" I stopped at the kitchen and called to the dog. He came to me.

I had avoided the beach since my accident there, but today I took the long way down the cliffside. Muldoon was always near.

When we reached the spot where the logan stone had crashed to the beach, I stood back. I gazed at it with horror. But something compelled me to go closer.

"Come, Muldoon," I called, but the wolf-hound hung back, whining, as I stepped nearer the rock to examine it minutely.

What do you expect to find after such a long time? I asked myself.

"It's just a rock, Muldoon." I patted the stone. "A very ordinary-looking rock." Muldoon whined again, and I glanced over my shoulder as I experienced a sensation of being watched.

"How I wish you could talk," I said to Muldoon. "Perhaps you are the only one who knows the secrets that hide here."

The logan stone revealed nothing to me, and I walked toward the precipice from which it had fallen. A hundred feet up, weeds had mended a jagged tear in the cliffs edge, but I could imagine how the logan had been situated. I climbed up the almost vertical cliffside a short distance to a small ledge, where I flopped down to rest. I smelled rain in the air, but the clouds seemed no more threatening than they had when I sat on the terrace eating.

Muldoon whined again and headed back toward the narrow trail we had taken from the top of the moor. I had had enough of this eerie spot. I scrambled to my feet to follow him, and as I did so my foot dislodged a boulder, which plunged down to the sea. I watched its descent. Then when I glanced back at the niche from which it had fallen, I saw a chunk of blue glass.

Picking it up, I examined it carefully. It was a glass setting too large to have fallen from a ring. It was only slightly scratched. I slipped it into my pocket, thinking that I would give it to Kimi to add to her secret collection of rocks and shells.

"Muldoon! Muldoon!" I glanced about, but the dog was gone.

The wind freshened, and I felt it plaster

my clothing to the contours of my body as I labored back up the cliffside. How ridiculous to have come here! I had done nothing but frighten myself, for I realized that I was trembling. I felt like a child who had scared himself with his own ghost story.

At the top of the cliff I looked for the dog. "Muldoon! Muldoon, come!" Muldoon had disappeared.

I headed for the manor, then changed my mind. My nerves were raw from the experience I had just put myself through. I didn't feel up to talking to anyone just yet.

Turning, I walked toward the stable. Perhaps a ride across the moor would calm me. I had not felt like mounting a horse since my fall, but now that all my muscles were healed, a ride would be no great risk.

Diablo snorted and stamped as I entered the stable through the door farthest from the manor. The stable was always gloomy inside, but now it was almost dark.

Moving cautiously, I found a lamp and lighted it. The acrid odor of the lamp oil blotted out the smell of hay and horses. Diablo still snorted and reared. Then he bucked, kicking the back of his stall with his hind legs.

"Easy, boy," I said in a soothing tone. "It's Genia I'm taking today."

What a horsewoman Angela must have been to have controlled Diablo! She must have had a will of steel and nerves of iron.

"Come, Genia." Attaching a lead rope to her halter, I led her from her stall and tethered her to a post. In the tack room I selected a fringed saddle blanket and a light saddle.

I lugged the saddle toward Genia and lowered it to the floor. I flung the blanket across the mare's sleek back. Then I struggled to lift the saddle onto the blanket.

Diablo was kicking and snorting in his stall, and now even Genia was protesting my attempts to saddle her. As I lifted the saddle she turned sideways out of my reach.

"Easy, girl. I'll fool you. I'll bridle you first."

I ran back to the tack room for the bridle, and when I returned I gasped in horror. The lamp! It had overturned, and tongues of flame licked across the loose hay blocking one exit.

The other door! There was still time to lead the horses out the other exit. I ran toward Genia, my fingers fumbling at the lead rope, just as Diablo crashed through the gate of his stall. Genia's whinny escalated into a scream.

"Diablo! Genia!" I shouted above my rising panic.

Rearing, snorting, pawing, Diablo flattened his ears and bared his teeth as I approached. Terror glazed his eyes as he struck at Genia with his forefoot, opening a gash on her withers. I dared not approach.

Flames blocked one exit, and the terrified stallion blocked the other. I tasted ash in the air as the burning hay crackled and sparked. Heat seared my face and arm. I choked on black smoke. I was trapped.

CHAPTER THIRTEEN

The inside of the stable was a nightmare of orange flames and black smoke. I crawled over the side of Genia's stall, then fell choking to the hay. I lay there gasping until I heard the flames licking at the wall of the stall.

I held my breath. I stood and climbed over the next wall into Diablo's quarters, again falling to the floor and trying to suck in fresh air.

Both horses screamed and lunged, then Diablo rushed back into his stall. His hooves were inches from my head as he pawed and stamped, but I was almost past caring. It would be less painful to die from a blow on the head than from burns.

I had all but given in to my fate when I heard someone shout my name. Who could know that I was in here? The smoke was so suffocating that I could not gasp enough breath to answer.

"Margo! Margo! Where are you?"

The voice spluttered and choked. Dan! Was he here to save me or to murder me? Above the roar of the flames and the snorts of the horses I heard thunder, but I knew that even a downpour would be too late to put out these flames.

Suddenly a boot clumped down inches from my head. Dan was in the stall, struggling with Diablo. I could have reached out and touched him, but he frightened me as badly as the fire. Then his foot kicked my leg, and he stooped to investigate.

"Margo! Thank God you're still alive! Can you hear me?"

He wasn't going to kill me. My hope surged. "Dan," I whispered. I couldn't speak, but I coughed and spluttered. Dan forced Diablo from the stall and led him out the door. Then he returned for me. He tried to carry me, but it wasn't necessary. Just knowing that Diablo was outside and that the exit was clear gave me the incentive I needed. I plunged to freedom.

"Good girl, Margo!" Dan followed me, leading Genia by one ear, and moments later the stable roof collapsed with a crash that shook the moor. I managed to stay on my feet until Tillie arrived, and then I fell into her arms.

"Miss Margo! Miss Margo!" Tillie cried. "Your poor arms. And your face. If only I had seen the flames sooner! I was in the kitchen fixing Sir Henry his afternoon gelatin dessert and —"

"Let's get her to the house, Tillie."

Guilford's voice rang in my ears, and I saw Dan step into the background as Guilford appeared on the scene. I wept with relief and perhaps from pain, but I smiled at him through my tears.

"I can walk," I said. "You needn't carry me." With Guilford's support on one side and Dan's on the other, I managed to inch back to the manor.

Vinegar Face and Katherine were waiting on the terrace, neither of them paying any attention to Kimi, who was watching the whole pageant with wide-eyed terror.

"I'm all right, Kimi," I assured her. "I'm all right, and Dan and the horses are all right. Show me a smile."

Kimi made a grimace that passed for a smile; then Guilford took charge once more.

"I'll help Margo to her room. Mrs. Foster, bring a soda paste and burn ointment. Tillie, take Kimi to the kitchen for a biscuit. And, Katherine, you go reassure Sir Henry that the fire has taken no lives."

"I must look a lot worse than I feel," I said, trying to put everyone at ease.

"You're badly burned," Guilford said.

Now that I could breathe again I experienced a sense of freedom and relief. The steel band binding my chest was gone, and I hardly felt the burns that had seared my arms and legs.

"Let's take these steps slow and easy," Guilford said.

I obeyed. Guilford left me at the door to my suite, and when I stared into a mirror I gasped and blushed. My clothing hung in half-burned shreds, my hair was singed, and dirt and soot blackened my skin.

"But I can move," I said aloud. "I can care for myself."

By the time Vinegar Face appeared with the ointment, I had removed my charred clothing and slipped into a loose sleeveless robe. I was unfamiliar with first aid for burns, and I washed myself in spite of the mounting pain. Vinegar Face had left my door open, and Guilford heard my gasp as she began applying the medicine.

"Don't be so rough." Guilford dashed into my sitting room and grabbed the ointment from her hands. "You're dismissed. Go!"

Such a look of astonishment crossed Vinegar Face's features that I almost laughed. But when fury replaced astonishment, foreboding chilled me. Vinegar Face was in love with Guilford. There was no doubt in my mind. I hoped my feeling for him was less obvious than hers.

With a flounce of her green uniform, Vinegar Face left the room, and Guilford applied the soda paste and ointment to my burns.

"I really feel better than I look," I assured him.

"Perhaps you're in shock." Guilford's eyes clouded with worry.

"I'm not in shock. I have a few burns, but none of them are serious. I'm the luckiest girl alive. Alive! An hour ago I wouldn't have given you two cents for my chances."

At that moment Tillie passed my doorway carrying a tray.

"Tillie," I called, "did Sir Henry eat his gelatin?"

"No, miss. I tried to get him to take it, but ye know. He wants his Angela."

"I'll take it to him." I rose and stepped into the hallway. My skin felt as if it might crack and peel off, but I ignored it. Sir Henry ate so little that I knew this bit of gelatin was important to him. Over Tillie and Guilford's protests I carried the tray to his room.

"Angela! What's happened to you?" Sir Henry scowled. "Your hair! Your face and arms! I've warned you that your wild escapades would get you in trouble one day. I see that it's happened."

"I'm afraid I caused a fire." I spooned gelatin toward him. "I lighted the lamp in the stable, and I must have set it down carelessly. It fell over into the hay. The horses are safe, but the stable is in ruins."

"But you are safe." Sir Henry smiled. "You are all that matters to me."

As a result of my urging, Sir Henry ate all of his gelatin dessert and I felt a small glow of success as I handed the tray to Tillie, who had been waiting for me in the corridor. I returned to my rooms ready for a long rest. I don't know how long I dozed before someone knocked on my door. I rose from bed and opened it.

"Guilford! Come in." I stood back to let him enter, and the black look on his face warned me that something was wrong.

"I'm sorry," I murmured. "I know my carelessness caused the fire. But perhaps . . ."

"Don't be a fool, Margo." Guilford set a small box on the floor beside the chair he had dropped into. "You didn't cause that fire. I just returned from the stable. The stench of lamp oil was everywhere — even outside the doorway."

"How could you tell? Didn't the flames consume it?"

"Haven't you noticed that it's raining?" Guilford nodded toward my window. "A downpour. Too bad it didn't start sooner. But the flames are dead now, probably to the consternation of your would-be murderer."

"Murderer!" I gasped.

"Do you have any ideas as to who might have set the fire?" Guilford's face was a hard shell. His hazel eyes glittered. Just then I remembered the blue costume jewel I had found on the cliffside. It suddenly took on a vast importance in my mind, and I determined to keep my discovery of it a secret, even from Guilford.

"Anyone could have done it, I suppose," I said at last. "Anyone except Sir Henry and Kimi. But who hates me that much? And why?" Against my better judgment I repeated Tillie's story to Guilford, and I also told him about returning my mother's locket to Sir Henry.

"Let this go no farther," I begged. "I only mean for you to know about it."

"I'll tell nobody," Guilford promised.

Guilford was so quiet either from surprise or shock that I spoke again. "Do you think Dan murdered Angela? Does he seem like a murderer to you? Guilford, I didn't come here seeking an inheritance. I came out of love and respect for my mother. Now I'm terrified. What am I going to do?"

"Keep calm, Margo." Guilford tapped the box he had brought with him. "I've been to the storeroom. I've brought a new lock for your door. I'll install it in a moment, but first I think it's time that you know about Angela."

I sensed a rising urgency in Guilford's voice.

"I thought I knew all about Angela. What else is there to know? Sir Henry worships her. I believe Dan still yearns for her. Even the Lanriths mourn her passing."

"The Lanriths saw only what they wanted to see in Angela," Guilford said. "She showed them her charming side. But at heart Angela was a devil."

Guilford brushed the unruly lock of hair from his forehead, and his face lost all traces of its boyish quality. "Angela was the youngest of the Merton daughters, and Sir Henry spoiled her rotten. Oh, he made a pretense of disciplining her. He locked her in her room and all that. But Angela would climb down the fire rope and dash about the countryside. Sir Henry's method of punishment was little more than a joke to her. He knew it and he indulged her outrageously. Katherine was insanely jealous of Angela's place

156

in Sir Henry's affections."

"Angela would dash about on the moor?" I asked.

"The moor held little interest for Angela. She'd take the fastest car at the manor and streak into Exeter. There's where she met Dan. He used to be a news reporter there. Angela found his job fascinating; she chased him until he married her.

"After Dan and Angela married, they moved here. Sir Henry trained Dan to manage the estate. Sir Henry thought that by offering Dan a job here, he would be tying Angela to him with bonds too firm to break. But he was never more wrong.

"Angela was bored to bits with life here, just as she always had been. She started chasing. She would leave openly in a car about noon and stay until the following morning. The London gossip columns were full of her antics."

"She could drive clear to London and back in that length of time?"

"The way she drove, she could." Guilford scowled.

"What about you?" I asked. "You were only a foster brother. Did you escape her attentions?"

Guilford's angry flush answered my question. "Frequently I would find her waiting for me in my suite whenever she thought she could get by with it. Once she hid in the back of my car, and I didn't know it until I arrived in London. She made a wild scene over me, and she must have tipped off the papers; reporters were milling about my office when I arrived. The columns made a big thing of it. Sir Henry was furious. Dan raged. And my business associates demanded explanations. There was never anything between Angela and me. But I didn't blame Dan for his fury. He had every reason to murder his wife."

"Then why are you protecting him?"

"Because he didn't do it. Dan had every reason to murder Angela, but he lacked the intestinal fortitude. Dan's too weak for that sort of thing."

"I'd think you'd want to know for sure who did it," I said. "How can you stand to live here with the thought of Angela's murderer running at large?"

"I accept the theory that Angela's death was accidental. She thought that rules were made for other people. She tried to break the law of gravity, but instead she only broke herself against it. She sat on that rock just daring it to give way with her. And it did. It's as simple as that."

I thought of the glass stone I had found. I

had transferred it from my skirt pocket to the pocket of my robe. "It isn't as simple as that. Don't you know that you're under suspicion? At least with Dan you are. He thinks you're after Sir Henry's money. He thinks you put Angela out of the way so that you and Katherine would be the sole surviving heirs." I couldn't bear to tell him that Dan thought I was in danger from Guilford because now I might be included in my grandfather's will.

"Do you believe Dan?" Guilford demanded.

"No. Of course I don't believe it." I spoke without hesitation, and Guilford bent toward me and kissed me with a gentleness I had never dreamed possible. I responded in kind.

Then, to my surprise, Guilford pulled himself away from me and began changing the lock. When the original lock was off and the new one was on in its place, he handed me the key.

"Keep your door locked at all times. Promise me that."

I nodded. As Guilford left me, as he closed the door behind himself, I wondered if he had kept a key to my door.

CHAPTER FOURTEEN

Guilford had just left when Katherine knocked on my door.

"Coming to tea, Margo?"

"Please excuse me today," I called without opening the door. "I much prefer to rest in my room."

"As you choose."

I was fairly comfortable on the chaise longue, so I stayed there and dozed. Tillie wakened me when she brought me a special tea tray.

"Sit down a minute, Tillie." I motioned toward the couch.

"Thank ye, ma'am. Don't mind if I do. Ye must be fairly upset with all that's happened to ye . . ."

"The easiest way out would be to believe that all the frightening things that have happened have been accidents. Angela accidentally fell to her death. I was accidentally locked in Angela's room. My fall down the cliff was accidental, as was the fire in the stable. Believe and it shall be true."

"But it isn't true, ma'am. And ye know it."

I closed my eyes and tried to think.

"How did Katherine treat Angela, Tillie? Guilford told me Katherine was jealous of Sir Henry's love for Angela."

"That she was, ma'am. Katherine could never get enough of Sir Henry's attention while Angela lived, but now that Angela's gone, Katherine treats her father dreadfully."

My mind raced. Katherine — the woman who never had enough of anything, love or money. Maybe Katherine had murdered Angela. With her sister out of the way Katherine stood in line for more paternal attention as well as a larger fortune.

"What about Mrs. Foster, Tillie? She's in love with Guilford. She must have hated Angela. What about Charles Lanrith? Angela must have sought him out in her quests for male companionship. Perhaps she was done in by a thwarted lover."

"Drink your tea and try to relax. I'll be back for the tray later." Tillie escaped, and I didn't blame her.

My head ached. Everyone had a motive for murdering Angela. Even Sir Henry. How it must have pained him to have fathered such a wayward child. I hated to think him capable of murder, yet I wondered if his hallucinations about Angela

161

were caused by a guilty conscience.

I took aspirin and slept for a bit, and when I awakened I felt rested. I decided to go to Sir Henry's room for a short visit before dinner. I had to carry on as usual. If I let fear for my own safety drive me from the manor, Sir Henry would surely die. He would take food from no one else.

"Sir Henry?" I called through the open doorway.

"Come in, Angela."

When I entered Sir Henry's suite, I blinked at its brightness. Every light and lamp was on, and Sir Henry sat up in bed. At first I thought he was just sitting there with his head bowed, but when I drew closer I saw that he was working — writing. His eyes were on a sheet of paper on his bed table, and he was feebly scrawling words.

"Good evening, Sir Henry." I paused in his doorway.

"Margo!" Sir Henry looked up at me as he spoke, and his eyes brightened. I hid my surprise at being addressed by my name.

"I haven't seen you for so long that I thought you'd gone away." My grandfather smiled. "I'm glad you're still here. I've been trying to work on my book today."

Sir Henry dropped his pen, fumbled for it, and then let it go. Clumsily he pushed the paper he had been laboring over toward me.

"Take a look at it, will you? Tell me what you think."

I read the legend. The writing looked as if it had been done by a child, but I knew what effort must have gone into it.

"It reads well, sir. Does it please you?"

"It does."

Sir Henry relaxed against the pillows, exhausted from his efforts. I could hardly wait to tell the family that his mind was clear — for the moment, at least. But should I tell? Perhaps we would both be in grave danger if I did. Before I could reach a decision, he asked for a glass of cherry wine.

"Be sure it's the cherry wine, Margo."

"I'll get it for you right away." Smiling, I left him and hurried to the kitchen. I met no one on the way, and I decided to tell Tillie the good news.

"He has stamina, the old man has." Tillie wiped her hands on her apron front, and I noticed earring marks on her earlobes. Had the sound of my footsteps prompted her to hide them in her apron pocket? At first I thought nothing of it, but then a clear image of those earrings that I had seen briefly and on only one occasion popped into my mind.

The stones in Tillie's earrings matched the piece of blue glass I had found on the beach. I was sure of it. I felt the setting in my robe pocket, and as I made casual conversation, my mind played with its new discovery. Could the setting I found have belonged to Angela's murderer? Who had given Tillie the earrings? She had been rather secretive about that fact. I had to know who the gift giver was, and I decided to try for an element of surprise.

Looking at Tillie's ears, I asked, "Who gave you those earrings, Tillie?"

Tillie's hands flew to her ears, and then her face flushed.

"Ye think I stole them, Miss Margo? Has old Foster been spreading lies about me?"

"Of course I don't think you stole them." I was truly sorry to have embarrassed Tillie, and I tried for a light, teasing touch. "I was just curious as to who gave them to you. I thought that perhaps you had a secret boy friend."

Tillie flushed again, this time in pleasure. "No, Miss Margo. Miss Katherine gave me the earrings. She said she never wanted to lay eyes on them again. It was not my place to ask why."

Katherine! I turned my back and pretended to search in the cupboard for the wine Sir Henry had requested. I never doubted Tillie's words; she had no capacity for deceit. And her words made sense. Katherine was frugal. She threw lavish parties. She dressed in Paris creations. But that bit of show was to create her "successful author" image. In private life she reused paper napkins. She dressed her daughter in homemade clothing.

If Katherine had lost a pendant or a broach, her thriftiness would have prevented her from simply throwing away the matching earrings. But then, Katherine could have lost the setting that I had found in a completely innocent manner. It was difficult to imagine so elegant a creature as she climbing the cliffside with pick or ax and trying to undermine Angela's logan stone.

"What are ye hunting for, Miss?" Tillie stood by my elbow ready to help, and I put the earrings from my mind.

"Sir Henry wants the cherry wine before dinner," I said.

"Aye, I took it to Mr. Dan's room after lunch. I'll fetch it for ye."

"Don't bother, Tillie. You have enough to do right here. I'll ask Mrs. Foster to get it for me." I welcomed escape from the kitchen. All I wanted was to go back to my room and try to fit the new information I had gleaned into the puzzle of Angela's murder and the attempts on my own life.

Vinegar Face was nowhere to be seen.

"Mrs. Foster?" I called into the silent drawing room.

"Mrs. Foster!" I raised my voice, but there was no response.

"For heaven's sake! I'll get the wine myself," I muttered under my breath. I hated to face Dan alone, but surely a request for the wine decanter would be brief.

Dan's suite was on the opposite side of the corridor from Sir Henry's. I approached the door and knocked. No answer. I knocked again, louder this time. Still no answer. I heard no sound within the rooms. Gently I turned the doorknob and found the door unlocked. Pushing it slightly ajar, I called again.

"It's Margo, Dan. Sir Henry would like the cherry wine if you happen to have it." The carpet and draperies absorbed my words. Dan was out, but I saw the wine decanter on a silver tray on his desk.

Opening the door wide, I crossed the carpet to Dan's desk and picked up the wine. The weight of the tray cut into my burned hand, and as I winced, Dan's almost empty glass overturned, spilling a trail of red liquid onto the carpet.

Quickly I grabbed a napkin and knelt to blot the stain. The desk hid me from view, and when Katherine and Dan suddenly entered the room, I was too surprised to make my presence known immediately. They were arguing, and as Katherine raised her voice she closed the door behind them. I was trapped.

CHAPTER FIFTEEN

Katherine's words rang out, and I couldn't help hearing.

"Our engagement announcement will be in the paper tomorrow, and the wedding will take place in September."

"I won't go through with it," Dan said. "I've stayed here all these years, but I refuse to marry you. I won't."

"Oh, yes, you will," Katherine purred. "Because if you don't, I'll let it be known exactly what happened to Angela. You wouldn't want all of England to know you murdered your wife, would you?"

"You can't blackmail me into marriage," Dan said. "I don't love you."

"But I love you," Katherine replied. "That's the important thing. I've loved you ever since Garfield died and left me a widow with a baby to care for."

I cringed in my hiding place. I knew I had heard too much, yet I had to reveal my presence before Katherine and Dan discovered me. I coughed.

Katherine strode to the desk and glared down at me. "How dare you spy on us!"

Her face went livid.

"I didn't mean to spy," I whispered. "I came for Sir Henry's wine and . . ."

Silence. Utter silence. Katherine's eyes blazed, and as she glared at me I managed to stand.

"I knew the moment I laid eyes on you and your mother's locket that you had come here to make trouble, to claim your share of the Merton estate."

"That's not true. I came here to keep a promise."

"A promise that would result in Father's forgiving Wanda, welcoming her daughter into the family. I was present at Wanda's going-away scene, you know. I remember Father's exact words. And you dropped the locket into his hand, didn't you?" Katherine sneered.

I held the wine decanter in front of me like a shield.

"Well, now you know all about your aunt Katherine," Dan said. "You should be able to write an interesting article." Dan's voice oozed bitterness, and my momentary hope that he might rescue me from my plight died. I knew that my newfound knowledge of Katherine's blackmail scheme and Angela's murder placed me in danger, knew that I had been in danger all along. My only chance for escape lay in keeping a conversation going until Tillie or Vinegar Face came looking for me to feed Sir Henry.

It is strange what odd things pop into one's mind in a moment of crisis. All I could think of was a quotation from a long-forgotten history lesson: The best defensive is a strong offensive. I lashed out at Katherine.

"I understand now why you were angry when Dan and I went riding, why you made a tape of your typing. But I had no idea you were trying to force Dan to marry you." Then turning to Dan, I demanded, "Why are you letting her do this to you? Allowing yourself to be blackmailed won't solve anything."

Katherine stared at Dan. If she loved him, as she claimed she did, she had a strange way of showing it.

"Let me tell her the truth, Dan." Katherine hesitated, her head tilted in a taunting manner. She was like a cat toying with a mouse before killing it. But who was the mouse, Dan or myself? Perhaps Katherine was after two mice.

Katherine opened her mouth to speak again, but Dan held up a hand to silence her.

"Let me tell it my way, Katherine. At least

allow me that small favor."

Katherine leaned back against the door, blocking my escape route, and Dan began to speak. His eyes smoldered.

"It happened years ago," Dan began. "Angela had come home one morning from heaven knows where after being out all night. We had a terrible row, and then she locked herself in her suite and refused to see anyone."

Dan paced before continuing, and I silently thanked him for the time that was passing. Each second of delay was a gift.

"About teatime Angela opened her door. I heard her, but I ignored her. She ran downstairs and outside, and I knew she was going to the logan. I worked in my study.

"When Mrs. Foster announced tea, I went downstairs. Sir Henry was sitting at the fireplace with Guilford. I bypassed them and walked out onto the lawn. I saw Angela sitting on the logan. She was staring out across the sea and rocking on the balanced stone. I called to her, but she either didn't hear or she pretended not to hear. So I started to go to her."

"Why, Dan?" Katherine's voice shrilled triumphantly. "Why? Were you going to bring her in to tea, or were you going to shove her over the cliff?"

"I intended to bring her in to tea," Dan whispered. "Margo, you must believe that. I intended to bring Angela in to tea. I swear it. But instead I murdered her."

"Dan!" I took a step away from him.

"Oh, don't think I pushed Angela over the cliff. It was an accident. Angela hadn't heard me approach. The roar of the sea masked my footsteps. When I spoke, my voice startled her. She — she and her logan . . . pitched forward . . . onto the . . . rocks . . . below."

"And I saw the whole thing." Katherine laughed. "Of course if Dan had admitted the truth, I would have had no hold on him. But he was weak. The Bodrevy authorities thought Angela had been alone when she fell, and Dan was quite content to let the matter stand that way. But I loved him in spite of his weakness, or maybe because of it."

"So you blackmailed Dan into staying here." I shook my head as the string of events began to make sense in my mind.

"I let her get away with it." Dan pounded his fist on the desk. "I loved Angela, you know. In spite of all she had done, in spite of the way she treated me, I still loved her. When she was gone, everything was gone. Nothing seemed important."

"But Dan was important to me," Katherine said. "I was in love with him. Marriage was my price for silence. Dan has stalled long enough. Better for you, Margo Landon, if you had delivered your mother's locket to Sir Henry the day you arrived and gone straight home without staying to nose into my business."

Time was running out. Katherine had far too much at stake to let me go free. And Dan was in Katherine's power. He wouldn't help me. Where was Tillie? Where was Vinegar Face? I knew I could no longer depend on them to save me. My only chance was to act.

I could throw the tray of wine in her face and perhaps escape into the corridor in the confusion that resulted. But when it came to explanations, it would merely be my word against Katherine's.

Setting the tray back on Dan's desk, I fought the desire to fling it at Katherine. I jammed my hands deep into the pockets of my robe, and my fingers curled around the blue glass setting. A plan leaped into my mind. It was my only chance, and a wild one at that. I pulled the setting from my pocket and held it on my palm.

"Ever seen this before, Katherine?"

Again Katherine's face grew livid; I had placed her on the defensive. Carefully I pushed the glass back into my pocket.

"Dan, did you ever stop to wonder why Katherine just happened to be watching Angela on the day she died? Why wasn't Katherine downstairs by the fireplace waiting for Tillie to serve tea?"

I gave Dan no chance to answer, but plunged on into my fabricated accusation, which I now felt might be more truth than error.

"Katherine was watching Angela that afternoon because she had undermined the logan and her curiosity could be satisfied in no other way. She had to see the results of her labor with her own eyes. Katherine murdered Angela, Dan. Katherine murdered her and made you think that you were the guilty one."

Katherine took a step toward me, but I held my ground. "Your frugal streak gave you away, Katherine. The blue stone in my pocket fell from a matched set of jewelry, didn't it? Although you didn't know it at the time, you lost it while you were hacking away at the earth that supported the logan. For that's where I found it. Later, when you missed the setting, you were disturbed. Would someone find the stone and trace it to you? But you hated to destroy the matching earrings, couldn't bear to see them tossed away. So you gave them to Tillie. And you told her never to wear them at the manor."

"Is all this true, Katherine?" Dan demanded.

"Blackmail is the least of Katherine's sins, Dan," I heard my voice shrill. "She murdered Angela because she was jealous of Angela's place in Sir Henry's affections, because she wanted Angela's share of the estate, and because she wanted you."

Dan faced Katherine. Fury and hatred replaced the brooding expression he usually wore.

"Of course that's all a lie," Katherine said, trying to give a haughty laugh. "This girl is mad. How can you even think of believing her ramblings! Her mind's as foggy as Father's."

Katherine stepped closer to me once more, and I clutched the setting in my pocket. But this time Dan moved between us. Katherine inched back to block the entrance again.

"I believe Margo's story." Dan glared at his sister-in-law. "You always were jealous. Angela came first with Sir Henry, and you couldn't stand that. You hated Angela. And you hate Sir Henry for preferring Angela to you. And you hated Wanda, too. You hated them both — because they both had love. You had nothing but your writing, and you couldn't bear it."

"Lies!" Katherine shouted. "All lies!"

"Oh, but it is true, Katherine." Dan paced the room. "I won't flatter myself by believing you are truly in love with me any more than you were in love with Garfield Noel. You just want me because you want everything that was ever Angela's. You must have planned her murder for weeks — for months."

I gasped as Katherine grew wild-eyed and pulled a gun from her skirt pocket. The overhead light glinted on the blue-black barrel as she aimed it at Dan and me.

"Give me that setting, Margo."

I laid the blue glass in her hand, wondering what she would do next. A knock on the door interrupted Katherine's plans.

"Is Miss Margo there, please?" Tillie called.

Katherine motioned me to silence. I held my breath.

"Margo's here, Tillie." Katherine spoke calmly. "She and Dan and I are in conference; she'll be out in a moment."

"I have Sir Henry's dinner tray," Tillie said.

"You may go," Katherine said to me.

"But I'll be waiting for you when you've finished with your chore. I'll be waiting."

Holding the gun out of sight in the folds of her skirt, Katherine opened the door as if nothing out of the ordinary had happened. I didn't expect Dan to do anything. Years of living under Katherines thumb could not be thrown off in a matter of minutes. And Dan was still in shock from hearing the truth about Angela's death. We were both in Katherine's power. She had the blue setting. She had the gun.

I had no doubt that Katherine would use the gun. She would be waiting for me when I came out of Sir Henry's suite. She would kill Dan and me and perhaps herself, too, before her pride and egotism would allow her to be exposed as a jealous shrew and blackmailer. I shuddered as I stepped into the corridor.

CHAPTER SIXTEEN

Tillie's face lighted up like a lamp when she saw me. "Oh, miss! I've been searching everywhere for ye. I've tried to feed him meself, but it's ye he wants. Margo Landon, not Angela."

"His mind is clearing." I wanted to scream, to try to escape, but an escape attempt might do much harm. I didn't want to endanger Dan or Tillie.

Turning to Katherine, who was now holding the gun out of sight behind herself, Tillie spoke again. "Dinner will be late tonight, Miss Katherine. Mr. Guilford has gone to the village on an errand, and Mrs. Foster insists that we wait for him."

"That'll be fine, Tillie." Katherine smiled.

I tried to smile as I balanced the tray in one hand and opened Sir Henry's door with the other. Then as I closed the door behind myself, I felt a momentary flood of relief. For a few brief moments I was safe.

"Good evening, Sir Henry." Forcing a smile, I set the tray down. I arranged the small bed table in front of him. My mind was whirling.

"You didn't bring the wine," Sir Henry said. "But no matter. I'm hungry. I want to eat now."

I could sense Katherine and Dan waiting for me. They would be in Dan's suite, but the door would be open a crack. And Katherine would be watching. I would have no chance of escaping down the stairway before she could overtake me.

I held a spoonful of fish chowder to Sir Henry's lips, and he took it. While he ate he regaled me with a legend. As he talked I racked my brain for some means of escape that would endanger no one but myself.

I think I had known all along that there was only one way out of Sir Henry's suite that Katherine might overlook at least for a short while. The fire rope. The thought of it made me shudder, but there was no alternative.

Purposely dropping a spoon, I knelt to pick it up. I took time to investigate under the bed. I pulled the fire rope toward me.

I rose with spoon in hand. How could I ever arrange the fire rope without Sir Henry's knowing? But of course! A hot pack!

"Sir Henry, you've used your eyes so much today that they look red and tired. I'll fix a hot pack of towels."

"Yes, yes. That will feel good."

I soaked a towel in warm water, wrung it out, and gently placed it over his eyes.

"You might tell me another legend while you hold the pack in place." I groped for the fire rope, trying to make no noise. "Surely there must be many legends about the moor."

Sir Henry began to talk, and before the first towel had cooled, I had tied the rope around the leg of a massive desk in the next room. I opened the window.

Returning to Sir Henry, I took the cooled towel from his eyes and replaced it with a warm one. Now was the moment.

Sir Henry's voice droned on as I perched on the window ledge and peered into the black nothingness below. Gingerly I let myself over the ledge, grasping the rope, straining for a toehold in a groove between the rocks.

I gripped the rope with my hands and tried to swing free of the side of the manor, but I thudded into it with a jounce that made my teeth rattle. My arms seemed to have no strength, and the rope burned my already sore hands as I slid down it. Faster. Ever faster. The pain was so great that I lost my grip on the rope.

I didn't fall far, but the drop knocked the wind from me.

"Margo! Margo!" Sir Henry called as I lay

in the blackness on the ground. If I could hear him, Katherine could, too.

Forcing myself to my feet, I ran. Then I stopped. I couldn't run blindly onto the moor. Moving slower, I eased my way to the burned-out stable. From a familiar door I pointed myself in the direction of the Lanrith cottage.

As I glanced over my shoulder I saw a light in the window I had just escaped from. Katherine knew. I pictured her already dashing down the stairs. Would Dan try to delay her and give me more time to escape?

I laughed bitterly to myself. What choice did Dan have in the matter! Katherine held the gun.

I ran until my lungs felt as if they might burst, and then I stopped and listened. For a moment the call of an owl rang in my ears louder than the sound of the sea.

I had started running toward the Lanrith house, but I had no idea if I had stayed on course. What if I plunged over the cliff? What if I fell into one of the mine shafts that pocked the moor?

I dropped to my hands and knees and felt my way carefully before putting my weight down. Suddenly I paused. Why was I heading toward the Lanrith house? Katherine and the Lanriths were friends. I might be heading straight into a trap. I veered to the right, to where I thought the path to Bodrevy Village lay. The hope of ever reaching the village was like a fantasy, but an impossible goal was better than no goal at all. I struggled for my life.

I had been creeping on hands and knees for what seemed like hours when I heard someone behind me. I froze. Looking over my shoulder, I saw a dim light flashing an arc to the right and then to the left. In my terror I lurched to one side and floundered into a thicket of briers. The thorns pierced my body, and I bit my knuckles to keep from crying out. But I was lucky. The briers offered refuge. I flattened myself on the ground.

"Margo! Margo!" Katherine's voice floated eerily across the moor. "Margo, dear, come back. Sir Henry needs you."

I held my breath. I had no intention of letting Katherine trick me into revealing my whereabouts. The arcing light came closer. Closer. At last I had to breathe. The stench of dank, rotting soil filled my nostrils as I flattened my cheek against the ground.

"Margo? Margo, where are you?"

Peering between the brier branches, I could make out Katherine's figure as she held the flashlight. She inched forward cautiously, carefully, like a lioness stalking her prey. At last she stood just on the other side of the briers from me. She was so close that I caught the scent of her musky perfume.

I held my breath as Katherine turned to the right and continued her trek across the moor.

"Margo. Margo." Her voice faded into the distance.

As soon as I was sure that Katherine was walking away from me, I scrambled to my feet. Although Katherine's light grew dimmer and dimmer, I watched it as I headed in the opposite direction. Sooner or later I had to come to the Bodrevy path.

Now that Katherine was heading away from me, I grew careless. I walked upright. I hadn't covered more than ten yards before the ground beneath my feet gave way. I felt muck sucking at my ankles, my knees, my thighs. I tried to brace myself with my hands, but I was into the bog to my waist before I knew it.

Would I go in over my head? No, of course not. If I sank any deeper, I would throw my arms out and support my weight on them. But what if Katherine came and found me helplessly mired? She could push me under. If my body was ever found, my death would be considered an accident.

CHAPTER SEVENTEEN

After my first moments of utter terror passed, I realized that although I was mired almost waist deep in the bog, I was no longer sinking. I stood on something solid, but when I tried to lift my left foot, suction pulled my shoe off.

I shivered as I felt the cold muck against my stinging skin, and I imagined the look of the green ooze that encased the lower part of my body. The smell nauseated me.

Something slithered across my forearm as I rested it on the ground in front of me. My skin crawled. I had seen no snakes on the moor, but Dan had told me of Diablo shying at the sight of three adders massed into a slate-gray ball.

I braced my elbows on the ground and tried to heave myself upward, but the bog sucked me back into its maw. I lifted one foot and leg at a time. No results.

After resting for a few moments I had an idea. I leaned backward and pushed with my feet. I repeated these awkward movements three times and found myself a bit higher above the ground. Both my shoes were lost, but that was the least of my worries at this point. Lean. Push. Lean. Push. Little by little I inched farther out of the bog.

At last I gave one final twist and heaved my feet back onto the moor with a resounding slurp. So sudden was my release that I fell backward; it took me a few moments to regain my senses. I lay on the ground barely breathing. Had Katherine heard all the noise I made in the bog? I listened for her footsteps, but the only sounds were of the sea and the wind and a restless owl.

Mustering my courage, I tried to stand. My body sagged under the weight of the muck that encased it. I could barely move. Groping my way, I dragged myself back toward the brier patch that had protected me from Katherine's sight. When I reached it, I broke off a limb, stripped it of thorns, and began scraping the muck from myself.

My arms ached, but when I finished the job as best as I could, I felt pounds lighter. I could walk easier. I might even be able to run if the situation demanded it.

At this point I had no idea which direction might lead me toward the Bodrevy road, but I listened to the sea, then chose a course that led away from the sound of the beating surf.

Again I crawled on hands and knees, feeling the way before me. I had just stopped to rest for a moment when I heard footsteps.

Katherine! She had heard me after all. This time I saw no warning light, yet I heard the steps creeping closer, ever closer. My mind ordered me to run, but my body refused to obey. I could never outdistance Katherine. I would face whatever was to come right here where I was.

The fog swirled around me, making ghostly movements in the air, and I cried out in terror as something wet and cold touched the back of my neck.

"Muldoon!" I wept with relief.

Muldoon licked my face. He whined. When I didn't move, he nipped my filthy skirt in his jaws and tugged. Grasping his collar, I let him lead me.

Muldoon had been raised on this moorland. He knew where the danger spots lay. I felt more at ease than I had for hours until he began to howl.

"Quiet, Muldoon!" I tried to close his mouth with my hands. "Quiet!"

He continued howling in spite of my protests, but even a howling dog was better company than no dog at all. I had always pictured dogs sitting on their haunches when they howled. But not Muldoon. He never paused in his slow but steady pace, and at regular intervals he howled his lament into the fog.

I don't know why I assumed that Muldoon would lead me toward Bodrevy Village. It was wishful thinking, and my dreams were soon shattered. The sound of the sea grew louder and louder. The wind cleared the fog away for a moment, and the moon lighted the night. I gasped as I peered over the cliff's edge, the very spot where Angela had plunged to her death on the logan.

"So there you are," Katherine said, her voice calm yet triumphant.

I whirled to face her.

"You thought you could escape from me."

Muldoon growled deep in his throat. I could only think of how foolish I had been.

The moon shone full on Katherine's broad forehead, and she tilted her chin in a defiant gesture as she raised the gun and aimed it at me.

"I hate to do this, Margo. I tried locking you in Angela's room, and that didn't frighten you away. I tried giving you a tumble down the cliff, and I tried to destroy you in the stable fire. Surely this gun will stop you."

I tried to run, but terror froze me to the spot. I felt Muldoon lunge past me.

"Muldoon!" I heard the impact of his body against Katherine's. It happened so suddenly that she had no time to pull the trigger.

I thought for a moment that the scream I heard was coming from my own throat. But it was Katherine screaming, screaming as she catapulted to the rocks below.

"Margo!" Guilford ran to my side, and I fell into his waiting arms.

"Where's Dan?" I asked. "Did she kill Dan?"

I couldn't hear Guilford's answer, and I still don't remember much of what happened next. I think Guilford must have carried me to my suite, for I don't remember walking. The next thing I knew, Tillie was bathing me in lukewarm water and my sodden clothing lay in a heap on the bathroom floor. I tried to question Tillie, but she was in such a state that her answers were garbled.

"Mr. Guilford, he came in while she was out there hunting ye. We wouldn't have known at all if Mr. Dan hadn't told us the whole story. A hard story for him to tell, too, him not being so very brave and all."

"Then Dan's alive?" I sighed. "I was

afraid, afraid she . . ."

"No. No." Tillie helped me from the tub and wrapped me in towels, then brought a fresh robe and slippers. I was barely dressed when Kimi dashed into my room wild-eyed and frightened.

I put my arms around her.

"Mrs. Foster says Katherine's dead." Kimi looked into my eyes, but I could not read the expression on her face.

"I'm afraid it's true, Kimi." Moments ago I had been in a state near shock, but now I came alert. Kimi needed me.

"Your mother had an accident. Come sit on my lap and we'll talk about it."

Kimi snuggled to me, and I explained as gently as I could what had happened to her mother, sparing her the ugly details.

"I want to sleep in your room tonight," Kimi said when I paused. "Don't leave me alone. I don't want to be alone."

Kimi shed no tears. I would have felt more at ease if she had. It would have seemed more natural and normal.

"Of course, Kimi. Come. I'll tuck you in."

Kimi followed me into the bedroom. I turned back the sheets that I longed to crawl between myself. She snuggled down into the pillow, and I pulled the bedcovers up under her chin.

"It'll be this way always, won't it, Margo?"

"We'll see." I kissed Kimi on the cheek, left the night light burning, then closed the door behind myself. Tillie was still waiting in my sitting room.

"Thank you for everything, Tillie. I . . ."

"Mr. Guilford's in the corridor." Anger sharpened Tillie's features. "He wants to know can he come in."

"Have you and Guilford quarreled?"

"He stole my earrings. He had no right. He said they were evidence, but that's not so. They were a gift."

"Let him in, Tillie."

Guilford stepped into the room and dropped down onto the couch. He seemed ten years older than he had that afternoon.

"The authorities came from Bodrevy." He ground the words through his teeth. "I promised them that nobody would leave the manor. They'll return tomorrow. We'll have to answer questions."

"Where's Dan?" I asked. "Are you sure he's all right?"

"Yes, he's all right. You were the one in danger, because you were the person Katherine feared and hated. She knew all about your returning Wanda's locket to Sir Henry.

That simple act endangered your life. Katherine knew when Sir Henry accepted that locket that she would have to share her inheritance."

"But she had the blue jewelry setting," I said. "It was my only evidence of murder."

"You had her figured out correctly, and she didn't want you to take your story to Sir Henry or anyone else. She knew you had charmed the old man and that she would be hard put to explain away your accusations. It would be easier and safer to put you out of the way. Of course, it would have appeared to be an accident. For who could have proved that you hadn't been lost in a bog?"

"Who told you what had happened?" I asked.

"Dan. When I returned from Bodrevy, you were gone. Katherine was gone. I happened to see Dan out on the moor. He was hunting for you. Give him credit for that, Margo. He was trying to protect you. I persuaded him to come to the house with me, persuaded him that he would have a better chance of finding you if we put Muldoon on your trail. That's when Dan told me the whole story. You and Tillie were the ones in real danger."

"Tillie?"

"Tillie. Because she still had the earrings.

I knew Katherine would be crazed with rage at having blundered in so small a detail as a pair of earrings. I took the earrings from Tillie and told her to lock herself in her room and answer to no one. It was the only way I could think of to save her from Katherine after Katherine found you."

"But where were you? Muldoon . . ."

"The dog broke away from me. I couldn't hold him. I can never hold him when he's on a howling spree. But I forgot about that in my worrying about you."

Guilford kissed me, his lips warm and searching. I clung to him.

We talked until almost morning. When Guilford left my suite, I made myself a bed on the couch in my sitting room in order not to disturb Kimi.

I knew that I was as deeply in love with Guilford as he was with me. I knew that I had been brave in a time of crisis. I had taken action. I had ordered my own life. I was finished drifting. I had made more decisions in the last few hours than I had made in the rest of my lifetime. And each decision I had made had given me the strength to make the next one. I knew it would ever be so. For the first time in my life I felt equal to the task of creating my own future.